ETERNAL NIGHT SHIFT SERIES

ALEX

LENA NAZAREI

Design and distribution by Bublish
Published by Nurse Lena Books
ISBN: 979-8-89989-052-9 (paperback)

PROLOGUE

April 2021

Kate & Sorin,

I don't need to tell you that we're still waiting for your wedding. You know what the pandemic's done to frontline providers, humans and what it means for social events. So, it was postponed again today, and I see how upset you are. It made me want to do something for both of you, give you a gift of sorts. I loved that Rhys shared his story for us, how happy it made you and how close we all felt to him after that. So, I want to do the same.

I want to give you, and all those we love, my story. If Rhys can be brave enough to bare his darkness and face his fears, then so can I.

It's not all happy; actually, it's mostly awful. But, it's my real-life history and it's yours now.

I've been writing in journals since before it was considered self-care. I think I was always searching for answers, even before I knew what the questions were. The journals helped me get my thoughts and feelings out in a way that was safe and helped me keep my head clear. I have them all in a box under my bed. I don't know if I'm really ready to open that box (can anyone ever be really ready to process trauma) but I need to so I can tell you everything in an accurate way and I'm committed to doing this. I plan to read them and incorporate the important points, so you get a full narrative of what led me to you.

You can't really step forward until you let go of what's behind you. We're in a new chapter of our lives now. It's still wild to think that the little boy who started that very first diary was destined to be an immortal warrior. The doctor in me has a hard time accepting that fate is a real force but it's getting harder and harder to ignore. I mean, all the work we do to save people… is it all useless? Is their fate decided before they get to us?

As much as I don't want to revisit my past, I know I need to do this.

I don't just give you my blessing to publish this but insist. You did a great job of hiding our true identities in your stories, so I feel safe putting this out there. I really think it'll help people to read this… know they aren't alone and that coming from a terrible beginning doesn't doom your future. You can't choose who you come from, but you can choose what you do with the cards you're dealt.

I'm getting ahead of myself.

I've been thinking about where best to start. I was born in Bedford, as you know. Sheena was seven when I was born. I think she was more excited for me to arrive than my own parents. As far back as I can remember, they were cold to us. My mom was basically on auto-pilot and my dad was either angry or absent. It was a normal upbringing for the late 70s, early 80s. Kids played on the streets until dark and a mall was the coolest place to hang out with friends.

So, here we go.…

PART ONE
CHILDHOOD

1986

My 8th Birthday

The sounds of children screaming from plastic tubes were mixed in with parents on the periphery complaining to each other about their lives. Under the din you could faintly hear a family singing happy birthday with all the excitement of a man on death row eating his last meal. The smell of fries was so strong that I think the salt was entering my blood stream through my nostrils, but it wasn't strong enough to not know that someone had vomited recently, and it hadn't been cleaned up well. I hated this party more than anything in recent memory and wanted to hide until it was over. I'd begged my parents for an outdoor party in the evening with a bonfire like Ricky Barnes had last month. Everyone had come to school after summer break and talked about how awesome it was. I'd known then, if we did the same thing, then all the kids would come. But my parents had said late September wasn't the right time of year for it and that *everyone loved McDonald's*. And that's the moment I'd realized adults could be stupid too, because no one loved a McDonald's party. This was made clear by the fact that no one had come to my party, and I was spending my third year in a row at a birthday celebration with only my sister and Norman.

Both attendees had to come.

Norman had to come for two reasons: he was my best friend, and his mom was my mom's best friend. Sheena had to come because if she didn't, my parents wouldn't let her go out this weekend. I liked to think she came out of love but knew better. She hated this place more than me. First, she said the air was full of grease and she got pimples just by looking at it and second, she'd decided that eating animals was wrong.

I was in the portion of the plastic tubes where the fishbowl glass bows out, allowing you to look down on the chaos below, when a small girl elbowed me out of the way to scramble past and snapped "Move it, fatso."

I'd fought back tears for the thirteenth time.

If I hadn't seen Sheena waving at me to come out, I think I would have started contemplating faking my death. Instead, I maneuvered past a large boy with snot streaming out of his nose to find the slide and descend to my sibling. A squeal fought past my determination to not have fun when she grabbed my ankles and pulled me into the blinding lights. The tickling that followed was fun until it was painful. Before I could verbally accost her for treating me like a little kid, she pulled a wrapped gift from her back pocket.

"Got you something, twerp. But you have to hide it and open it in the home. You can't tell Mom and Dad, capeesh?"

"Capeesh," I managed while recovering from the abdominal spasms that follow a tickle session and full laughter, especially when your only idea of exercise is trying to save Princess Peach on Nintendo.

Sheena looked around to make sure we weren't being watched and excitement slid through my body with the thought of doing something we shouldn't. The rectangle package was slapped into my palm to be quickly transferred to my pants' pocket. The weight of it sent a thrill across my nerves and burned in its fabric prison for the rest of the party. Even the lackluster cake and seeing only one present on my table didn't destroy my joy. I had complete faith in my sister's choice of gifts. She gave the best presents in front of my parents so I couldn't even imagine how cool a gift had to be to be kept secret.

The station wagon journey felt like a lifetime. I gave the occasional "yeah" to everyone as they discussed the party and how much fun it was. I think they'd needed just as much convincing as me to believe it wasn't the saddest event in history, but I didn't care. I just wanted to open that present.

I couldn't say anything to Norman since he was riding home with us, but I kept winking at him to indicate I'd have a good story later. Looking back, and remembering his confusion, he may have thought I had a facial tic or was hitting on him but back then I was sure he knew what I was trying to tell him. The second the car was in the driveway, I was running into my house and yelling back to my best friend that I would come over later. I knew my mom would walk him across the street and start drinking with his mom. My dad would go into the garage, turn on music, light up a pipe and start some kind of woodworking. My sister was already walking down to the corner where someone would pick her up and she'd be home either in an hour or two days. So, I was alone.

Checking the lock on my door three times to ensure it was engaged, I dropped to the carpet and pulled the package from my pocket. Before I could rip into it, I saw the gift on my bed. Grabbing it, I put the brightly wrapped contraband on the floor. The paper was no match for my fingers and what lay in my palms within seconds was the coolest thing I'd ever possessed. My dad had plenty of music albums, but they were all records. He didn't see any reason to start buying cassettes and would never let me even talk about my own radio. But all the kids in school talked about their tapes and the music they'd listen to in their rooms. One of the reasons everyone had loved Ricky's bonfire party was the massive boombox and all the cassettes his parents had gotten him.

I'd wanted my own tape more than anything. And now, in my chubby hands, was my very own music tape by a band called Aerosmith; the gift on the bed had been a Walkman. I couldn't even begin to understand how she'd bought them or gotten them wrapped and into my room without anyone knowing, but I didn't care. These two items would be my most prized possessions well into adulthood. I'd listened to the tape so many times that it's finally worn out.

Later that night, I'd smuggled it over to Norman's and we'd hidden in his tree house to listen to Aerosmith for the first time, bonding over the shared musical experience. We'd never heard rock before that, and I think that moment awakened something inside us. I don't know if it was rebellion per say, but it was definitely some kind of determination to push back against what my parents wanted for me. Listening to the electric guitars and screaming lead singer I knew two things: I wouldn't stay in Bedford for longer than I had to, and I loved my sister more than anyone in the whole world.

2

1984

The Summary Before 5th Grade

It hadn't been the first time that I'd been afraid Sheena wouldn't come back. The fight with Mom and Dad had been really bad that time. I'd been sent away before the worst of it had happened. However, being curled up in bed, under the blanket, hadn't blocked out the sounds of slaps and yelling. As always, my mom had stayed quiet. All the screaming was from Dad and Sheena. I was pretty sure my sister hadn't hit my dad, so she'd been on the receiving end of all that violence. When I was smaller, I'd been confused about why he was always so mad. Then, I got older and wanted him to stop hurting my sister. That night, I'd wished he'd just disappear forever.

I'd stopped hoping my mom would do something a long time ago. She'd always just sit in the corner and watch. To me it was like she was agreeing with what he did, like she was a silent cheerleader. She never reproached him or comforted Sheena after. She'd just play audience and then go stay busy in the kitchen. It got to the point where the smell of baking cookies filled me with dread. It took me years to stop associating hot food smells with fresh bruises and washing blood off my face. On Sundays, when I'd been forced into bible classes, I'd sometimes pray that God would make my dad nice. We'd color pages and make crafts that matched the religious story they'd told us that day. The other kids would proudly show their parents, but I would just leave it in the classroom to be thrown away. It all felt so pointless. How was a crayon and a picture of a lamb going to make it all better?

Staring out the living room window had only made me feel more isolated. The street was full of kids on bikes and every other porch held adults drinking tea and laughing. Mom and Dad were across the street with the Crawfords, their best friends. Mrs. Crawford and my mom hadn't really talked until they were both pregnant together. Norman Crawford and I were born the same week. One of my first memories was in their backyard. Norman and I splashed in a blow-up pool while the moms giggled and whispered. I can still smell the oil they put on their skin to tan with and hear the radio playing. I must have been four and it's one of the few, happy memories I still have.

Norman was my only friend, and he was away at camp, so I was stuck inside. Witnessing the children who jumped through sprinklers without a care in the world, I felt a bubbling hatred for those happy kids. I bet their parents never hurt them and they got popsicles all the time. I bet they had lots of buddies who they slept in backyard tents with, and they never had to imagine their sisters running away. I watched my parents sip at their drinks, pretending everything was fine.

Looking back now, I think they were hoping Sheena didn't come back. I think, if they'd had their wishes, I'd run away, and they'd have no kids. Even better, they'd get all the sympathy and people would bring them casseroles and they'd be happy. My ten-year-old brain couldn't understand why people would have kids if they didn't want them but as an adult I would look back and land on a theory. They'd had kids because that's what they were supposed to do. They were supposed to go to church and buy a house in the suburbs and have a boy and a girl. When they'd done it and still hadn't been happy, they'd blamed us. I think they thought we hadn't been good enough to make them happy, that we'd failed them when our mere existence hadn't satiated their own unquenchable need for something to bring them bliss.

My birthday had been a few months away, but Sheena had given me my gift early this year. I'd thought she just couldn't keep it hidden anymore but now I think she'd somehow knew a lifechanging event was coming. Something had told her to give it to me now, that I'd need it.

The leather journal was the same blue as my eyes and came with the fanciest pen I'd ever seen. The edges of the pages were shiny gold. It laid in my lap while I watched the sun set at the end of the street, the porch lights turn on and the kids start to chase fireflies. Still, Sheena hadn't returned.

When I opened the stiff pages of the diary, the smell that rose from it was similar to the school library. The crispness of the paper told me it was brand new, but it felt somehow old and priceless. I wondered how she'd gotten it but probably didn't want to know.

I was a little sad to write in it, ruining the pristine whiteness of the perfectly, unbent and unused pages. However, once I started to write, I couldn't stop. Words poured out of me when they were set free from their prison in my chest. When she'd handed me the journal, I'd though it was an odd choice. Obviously, I'd acted excited but didn't see why she'd given me a diary. I thought diaries were for girls. But, now that I was writing in it, I could see the appeal.

Even as I wrote, I'd known this thing needed to remain a secret. If he or my mom found what I was writing, it'd get the pounding of a lifetime. It was worth the risk, though. It felt way too good to get all of this out of me and onto a page.

My first journal entry started with the previous night's events. Sheena had been washing the dishes and I'd been drying. Even though it was a chore, I loved this time with her. She'd tell me these made-up stories about fairies in the trees and dragons in the skies. Sometimes, she'd stop the story and let me finish it. I was never as imaginative as her, so my endings were always terrible, but she'd give me these huge reactions, pretending my part of the story was thrilling to her.

That night, I was really getting into it. My ending involved a giant rising from the lake to chase the fairies. While mid-toweling, I threw my hands up in the air. The plate I'd been drying flew from my grip. I watched in horror as the dinnerware sailed up towards the ceiling and plummeted to the floor. My scream was what alerted my father, but it was the crashing sound that got him out of his chair. Stomping headed our way with a speed that sent my every nerve on fire. There was no time to clean up the mess and I knew it didn't matter. Us breaking something was the greatest sin according to the book of my father. He saw us ruining anything in the house as a direct insult to him and blatant disrespect of his hard work.

My little brain was working frantically, running every option through my head. But I couldn't think of a single excuse that would be sufficient.

He turned the corner and filled the doorway of the kitchen; his belt already pulled from his jeans and folded in his hand.

"I'm sorry, Daddy," shot out of my mouth before I realized my sister was also talking, trying to take the blame. He looked between the two of us and then down to the shattered plate. What I saw in his eyes when his gaze raised from the floor to me, made my bladder threaten to empty itself. He had covered the distance and had my arm in his grip before I knew what was happening.

I'd seen him hurt Sheena so many times by then, but truly believed he'd never do it to me. I think a part of me believed what my dad said, that she made him do it. But that moment, as he squeezed my arm so hard, I thought it would snap, I knew my time had come.

My body shook so violently from fear, that I thought my heart would stop. His belt was raised in the air, and I closed my eyes, bracing for the strike. Shockingly, the crack of the belt didn't result in pain. I opened my eyes and saw why. My sister stood between me and my punisher. A red streak was lighting up across her shoulder and back. "It was me," she screamed into his face. "I broke the plate, you fucking psycho. Don't touch him." She pushed herself backwards into me and the pressure pulled my arm from my father's grip. She whipped around to me. "Go to your room, Alex. Now." I froze for a moment, not wanting to reward her sacrifice with my retreat. I wanted so badly to be brave and stand by her side with her. But I was too scared.

I ran crying into my bedroom and found safety under my Ghostbusters blanket. We'd found it at a church flea market, and I'd been thrilled. The Real Ghostbusters was my favorite Saturday morning cartoon. My mom didn't like anything with ghosts or goblins, she believed it was stuff from the devil and cartoons were trying to pull children away from God. I'd once had to sit and read the Bible for one hour after she caught me watching Scooby Doo. She'd also believed that the devil used music and video games and books and a thousand other things, so I was pretty much used to her lectures and punishments. But, for whatever reason, she'd caved and gotten me the comforter. It's what I laid under as I'd listened to Sheena scream in pain over and over yet still hold her ground and call him an asshole. The resulting slaps sent me into tears but were nothing compared to the slamming door that announced she'd left again.

Now a day had passed, and I still didn't know where she was. She'd been gone before. One time, she'd asked to go to the mall and my dad had said yes. She'd called that night to explain it was a mall in New Jersey and she'd be home in two days. I'd thought my dad would throttle her that time, but he'd laughed and told me "I guess next time I should ask what mall." Then other times he'd beat her for being a minute over curfew. That was my dad, you didn't know what would lead to a beating and what would lead to praise.

But this time had felt different. This time, I knew in my gut, there was a real possibility she'd run and never look back.

It wasn't like I'd actually been told the truth about what had happened either. My mom and dad had told me one thing, then told their friends another. I'd even heard my mom on the phone to the pastor, telling a third story, asking for prayer and sympathy. She'd made eye contact with me and for a brief second, I feel like I'd seen shame in that gaze, then she'd turned away and continued the narrative into the receiver. And none of those stories felt like the whole truth. All I wanted to know was if Sheena was coming back but only time could tell me.

After the third day, I'd cried myself to sleep.

That night at dinner, Dad and Mom had told me that she'd run off with a boyfriend to a concert in a different state. I heard them later talking to the neighbors, saying she'd been kicked out of school and was wild. I'd been filled with more emotions than my human form could house. I didn't want to believe any of what they said. I'd been sure that I'd known my sister better than anyone but was having to face that maybe I didn't. The reality that my sister had a whole life I didn't know about was sinking in fast. With all of that knowledge came the certainty that she wasn't going to be my father's punching bag any longer. Even though I was trying to talk myself out of it, I knew deep down that someday she'd leave and not come back.

As days turned into weeks, I'd had to face the truth; my sister hadn't gone to a concert. She'd left willingly and hadn't taken me with her. My protector had finally protected herself. I understood why she'd left, couldn't be upset with her, but was terrified for what it meant for me.

Several people had asked my parents what I'd wanted to – why didn't you call the police? Days 1-4 they'd told everyone that she was at a concert, she'd done this before and would come back. Days 5-10 they'd told everyone that she was a "troubled child" and just needed a life lesson. They'd been certain she'd return when she saw how hard life was alone. Days 11-14 they'd just asked for prayers, stating that she was taken in by those who listened to rock music and worshipped the devil and needed Jesus. They'd expressed that only the Lord could save her now. They'd enjoyed all the attention and hugs at church and donations to support them in this "difficult time." Finally, after two weeks, they knew they'd have to include law enforcement or face accusations that they didn't care about their daughter.

Unfortunately, it turned out that police cared less about a missing teenaged girl than her parents. The two officers had listened to my parents' story about Sheena's last night (one totally different from their previous versions) and said that teens ran away all the time and my sister would probably come home soon. They hadn't talked to me, neighbors or teachers to get a picture of the home life. Instead, the policemen had scribbled in a pad and chalked the whole thing up to a young adult who wanted to be free.

No one had put up flyers with her picture or called the news. They'd just shrugged their shoulders and treated my missing sister like it was no big deal.

So, I'd packed a duffel and planned my own escape; I'd run away one night and jump on a bus. Then, I'd just start looking for her. In my naïve mind, I believed that people would see a ten-year-old and take pity on them, be more likely to help because I was young. I'd been certain it would be like the movies; I'd stumble across a jaded detective who'd lost hope in the world, but he'd see me and want to help find Sheena. Then, we'd work together to find my sister. In my imagination, this detective would actually find her and then adopt us. We'd live with him in Los Angeles and be happy.

The night my sister had shown up in my window, I'd had that packed bag below my bed. One word and I would have climbed through my window and run away with her into the night.

But, instead, she'd fled and left me again.

When it happened, when Sheena had tapped at my window only to say goodbye and run, I'd believed I hadn't earned my freedom yet. My little mind had believed I was left to be my father's whipping boy because she'd done it for so many years and now it was my turn. I'd thought if I'd gotten hit a magic number of times, she'd suddenly return to take me away.

Only time and wisdom would give me clarity.

As I write this and look back, I'd known that night that something had been changed in her. Obviously, I couldn't possibly have guessed what it was, but I'd known something was profoundly different. However, I was so overcome by having her for only seconds and then losing her again that I couldn't focus on anything else. Over the next few weeks, I'd split my energy between trying to convince my parents that she'd been there and replaying the interaction with her in my mind. I didn't sleep for days at a time, sitting at that window, waiting for her to return, holding my duffel in one hand and a flashlight in the other.

My parents tried to convince me it had been a nightmare, that the mix of stress and exhaustion had led to me hallucinating my sister at my window. When I wouldn't let it go, they made me talk to our pastor who just recommended Bible passages for me to read and made me promise to pray at bedtime.

I didn't.

As the summer transitioned into autumn and I started fifth grade, I was told I had to visit the school counselor, Mrs. Evans. Every Friday, during lunch, I'd go to the counselor's office to talk about my feelings. For months I'd try to explain the night with my sister to Mrs. Evans in the hopes the counselor would believe me and help me find Sheena. By Christmas, I'd stopped telling the story to her just like I'd stopped telling it to my parents, the church, my teachers or anyone else that asked. I'd repeat the official tale that my sibling was just another statistical runaway and nod while they told me how bad they felt for me. Only Norman and my journal heard my true feelings because they were the only ones that believed me.

3

1989

5th Grade & Beyond

It was six months after Sheena disappeared that my father hit me for the first time. My hand shook as I wrote down the events leading up to that inevitable moment. There was a part of me that had been hoping for that first smack to just get it over with. The fear and anxiety of knowing it would happen, but not when, was worse than just being hit. I'd been witness to the abuse so much that I believed watching was worse than being on the receiving end. When he finally connected his open palm to my face that night, I'd been shaken but also relieved to know what I would be in for. I'd been foolishly certain that I could take this abuse for my mom until either turning 18 or rescue from my sister took me out of the house forever.

I'd been too young to understand that the first strike was only him breaking some kind of hatred seal and he'd only been warming up. I think he'd convince himself that Sheena was the sole reason that he ever flew off the handle. He'd believed that there was no evil in him and his wicked daughter had brought out the worst in him. Once he'd snapped and hit me, it was like he'd finally given up that hope and accepted that he was a monster, so he wasn't going to hold back anymore.

Eventually his hand wasn't open anymore and his slaps turned to punches. First, he'd punch my back or my belly, then make a snide remark about how soft I was. Then his single punches turned to him hitting me until he was tired. Then he'd stopped caring about hiding the abuse and would punch me wherever he felt like. I was 14 when he'd given me the first of many black eyes and split lips. No one in school, at church or around the neighborhood asked about it and I was saved from having to lie.

When I started puberty and start to show signs of becoming a man, his hatred of me only increased. I think deep down he was so miserable in his life that the mere thought I may become the man he wasn't, enraged him. Once I started to work out and build muscle, the burning started. Unlike the beatings, which he had no shame for, he only put his cigarettes out on my skin when my mother was gone or passed out. It was like he wanted to ruin me the way he felt ruined.

Truthfully, the physical abuse wasn't the worst part, it was the psychological games that did the most damage.

Anytime I'd try to talk about Sheena, he'd shut down and pretend he didn't know what I was talking about. My mother would reach into the cabinet above the stove to pull out her liquor and shuffle to the back porch to drink her thoughts away. Within four hours of the mention of my sister's name, my father would've found a reason to hit me, and my mother would be in the hammock, ignoring the sounds of my torment. It was a price I was willing to pay to continue saying her name, keep her memory alive and hold onto the hope that she'd come back for me.

Every person who'd ever known her had slowly erased her from their reality.

But I never relocked that window and that packed duffel bag stayed under my bed until I graduated high school.

4

1996

Senior Year

I'd had just enough time to grab a Pop-Tart before Norman would leave me behind and I'd have to ride the bus to school. My best friend had gotten a full gym setup in his garage for his 15th birthday, which turned out to be the best day of my life. His family had given me a house key to the side door by then, so he told me to use it anytime I wanted. Normally I'd get my workout in after classes, but I'd had trouble sleeping and decided to lift before school. Time had gotten away from me, and he'd busted into his garage when I was mid-bench press to tell me I had 20 minutes to shower and eat before his car left his driveway and I had no ride to school.

With hair still dripping, I'd snatched the silver-foiled pastry out of the cabinet and booked it across the street as he was pulling out. The car was rolling as I opened the passenger door and jumped in.

"Like you're not big enough, Kitchner, you gotta workout twice a day now?" Norman shouted over his radio. "What are you trying to prove, man?"

I laughed, seeing no reason to explain to him that I'd had another sleepless night.

He continued. "I'm just busting your balls. I'm sure my old man is thrilled it's getting used. I think he wishes you were his son instead of me."

"I doubt that's true," I assured my friend, even though I also thought it was true. Mr. Crawford had said more than once that he'd wished I'd rub off on Norman, that he'd do more weightlifting and less skateboarding. My friend couldn't help that he was 5'8" but I think his dad was hoping the gym equipment would encourage him to put some muscle on his 140lb frame. The kids in school had started calling him Spider when his growth spurt had made his arms and legs long and thin but not done much for his overall height. At first, he'd hated the nickname but now he embraced it. He'd even gotten a spider tattoo in some guy's basement last summer.

"It's fact and you know it. Not your fault though, or mine, just life." He cranked up the volume. While we drove and the bass thumped in my chest, I wished for the thousandth time that Mr. Crawford was my dad and the person driving was my brother. How different would my life be?

Before I could spend too much time in that particular fantasy, we pulled into a parking spot and the chaos that was our high school. It was the first day after winter break and the buzz in the air was the result of my class knowing they were only months away from graduating and getting out of this town forever. While I wasn't a fan of chaos, I couldn't blame everyone for being antsy. By May, I knew the hallways would essentially be the island from *Lord of the Flies* and I was determined to end my high school days without trouble, so I planned to lay low in the library from that day until we were handed our diplomas. I'd gotten accepted to every university I'd applied to with scholarships; I wasn't risking my ticket out for anyone or anything.

"Alex," the shrieking voice could only be one person, and I braced myself for what was to come. My begging look to Norman was met with smiling and a wink, then he left me to face my own consequence. As I turned to the squeal with a plan to nicely say hello and move along, Nancy barreled into me. Her leap landed my back against the car, and I barely grabbed her in time. Her legs were around me before I knew what was happening. "Baby," she repeated over and over in between kisses on my face and neck. Heat rose in my face, but she didn't seem to mind my embarrassment or the dozens of teens watching the show.

It was a small town, so I knew that everyone in our school was aware of what had occurred between Nancy and I over break. They were all at Zach's holiday party when we'd played 7 Minutes in Heaven. They'd seen me drink too much. They'd seen Nancy and I go into the closet. They'd witnessed us come out twenty minutes later and known what we'd done.

What they hadn't seen was the very confident Nancy take charge and encourage me to go "all the way." She was the hottest girl in school and very skilled at what she'd done. As far as first times go, it was not the worst way to experience such a thing. But I'd been awkward and nervous, she'd done all of the work and protected my masculinity by waiting an extra seventeen minutes before we emerged. I'd thought she'd be done with me after that and the worst scenario was that she'd tell her friends that "big, hot Alex was terrible in bed."

Instead, she'd fallen instantly in love and called my house 100 times over the school break. I'd manage to dodge the calls for the most part, but a handful of brief conversations had convinced her I felt the same way.

I did not feel the same way.

Setting her down onto the pavement, I smiled and tried to lightly push her away from me so I could grab the backpack I'd abandoned to catch her. "Hi Nancy. How was your Christmas?"

She allowed me to sling the bag onto one shoulder before she wrapped her arm around my waist and started to usher me towards the building. For a man who stood up to my father without fear, I was oddly terrified of this 5'3" cheerleader and what she was going to say when I told her that I didn't want to be her boyfriend.

Her words were drowned out by the sound of my heart pounding in my ears so when we reached the hallway and she looked up at me expectantly, I had no idea what the question was. I panicked and laid a quick kiss on her cheek before disappearing into the guidance office.

"Yes, Mr. Kitchner," the office secretary barked, clearly just as annoyed for the return of school as the students.

"I need to see Mrs. Callahan," I said more to the carpet than the woman in front of me.

A wave of the hand towards the back offices told me my counselor was in, and I was allowed to head back.

Mrs. Callahan's grey hair was twisted into a knot on the top of her head and several pencils stuck out of it. She must've had a dozen pairs of glasses because they were always different colors. Today's selection was a yellow that matched the sunflower painting on her back wall. They framed brown eyes when she looked up to see me and smiled. "Hey there Alex, what can I do for you?"

"I got into Brown." She jumped up, clapping her hands together.

"I knew you would," she beamed. "So, is that the one?"

"I don't know," I admitted. "I can't decide what to study and I feel like picking a major would help me choose a university."

"That's true," she dropped back to her chair. "But you don't have to know now, Alex. The first year is the same for everyone. You do your core classes. Maybe you need to just pick a school, then during that first year you can figure out what you like."

"No," it sounds harsher than I'd meant it to, so I soften my tone for the rest. "I don't want to waste time. I want to go into college with a plan and a path."

"Well, I get that. So, why don't you start doing some research? Start reading books on different subjects and see what gets you excited. You have some time before you have to tell one of those schools that you accept their offer."

"That's actually a good idea. I was already planning to hit the library more."

"Alright, then. Let me know when you decide, and I'll help you with all the paperwork."

I left her office feeling hopeful. I knew that one of those schools would be my way out of this town and my house. I kept telling myself it really didn't matter what I studied, just so long as I was free. But I meant what I said to Mrs. Callahan; I didn't want to waste time or take a chair from a college student who would do something worthy with it. So, I had a mission: decide what I wanted to do with this opportunity, get the hell out of town and never look back.

By lunch, I was practically jumping out of my seat and running to the library. I began in the first stack of the non-fiction section and started pulling out books that looked interesting. You were allowed to check out five at a time. My daily routine was the same: use my library time to peruse books, pick five that I wanted to really read and those were the ones who went home with me. Every night I'd read the books, finishing some and tossing others aside when it was clear it wasn't what I needed. Then, I'd return the five chosen books the next day to spend my lunch deciding on five more.

It went on like this for two months. If Nancy called, I'd tell her I was studying and hang up.

As the winter was thawing and the first hint of spring drifted through the air, I stepped out of Norman's car to see Nancy stomping towards me. With a wave a relief, I realized she was coming to break up with me. It went easier than I could have hoped. She told me she needed more attention. I told her she was right. She ranted about how I would leave in the fall for school and probably never answer the phone; I'd told her she was right. She cried and told me that I didn't deserve her; I told her she was right. Then she hugged me and disappeared into the crowd of rowdy seniors.

That was the day my journey through the stacks led me to the occult section. I felt ridiculous as I withdrew volumes about ghosts, aliens, spirit boards and past-life regression. Part of me rallied against this section, reminding myself that my time was dwindling. However, a quiet part pushed me forward into the unknown, like I knew a turning point was so close. As the librarian scanned my choices for the evening, her eyebrows arched. I didn't know if her response was because she thought I was a fool for adding this information to my already heavy thoughts or because she was also curious about the ideas. I worried for a moment that she would tell my parents I was checking out such material, but I was certain she wasn't in our church. If my mother knew I was bringing home occult studies, a fresh burn on my back was a certainty. Still, I put the books into my backpack and risked the consequence.

5

Dinner felt like an eternity as I waited for my father to finish his meatloaf so we could all be done. He'd trained us both well to not even leave the table for the bathroom until he rose and excused himself. I sat quietly, not wanting to draw attention to myself, while I felt the books calling out to me in my bedroom. I'd almost opened my bag and pulled them out as soon as I'd returned but it wasn't until after supper that I knew for sure my parents would be too tired to come into my room. The window between after-school and dinner always held the possibility of one of them entering my bedroom for a surprise search, reviewing my completed homework or starting a fight just so they could direct their frustration at me.

But, after dinner was always mine. They'd both watch TV until 8pm, then retire to their rooms to sleep. My mother had been taking sleeping pills for years by then and my father always had enough beer in him to knock out a horse, so I was free to breathe easy and not worry about intrusion.

When my father finished that night, he stood, and I mimicked the action. It was the first time he looked old and frail to me. I was at my adult height by then, well over six feet, and he was so much smaller. His years of working, drinking and smoking had given him hunched shoulders, leathery skin, thin limbs and a rotund belly. I had the overwhelming urge to push him over but quickly shoved the impulse deep down to be ignored.

Thanking my mother for dinner, I dropped the dishes into the sink to escape into my room with the usual homework excuse. I didn't know why I even made excuses anymore; they didn't seem to care what I did. They hadn't asked once about college.

Once the door was locked, I extracted my literary contraband and cracked open the first book. It didn't take long for me to know I didn't need to read another word of the first one since alien abduction was not a college major. The second book was even less helpful since I was pretty sure, at the time, that fairies didn't exist.

Book number three was innocuous in its appearance with its brown leather cover and simple gold block lettering. I'd grabbed it earlier in the day because I was out of time to choose, with only four tomes in my arms. It sat amongst the stories of "real" hauntings, so I was shocked to realize it wasn't about poltergeists. Its title was simple, but I hadn't read it until that moment: *Vampires*.

My clock told me it was midnight, and I still had three books to read. I could set this one aside and move onto the next since I didn't think there was a future in vampire studies. Still, I couldn't make myself put the book down. Something inside me was vibrating like I'd been electrocuted. With shaking hands, I opened the stiff pages and started down a path I could never have foreseen.

As the sun rose the next morning, I'd written pages worth of notes and planned to keep the book to read again the next night. The purpose for the books had been lost to another mission by the time I scooped my things into my bag and ran across the street. Norman was shocked by the condition I arrived in, but I ignored his questions about my unchanged outfit and unkempt hair. The moment he gave me the opportunity, I blurted out my findings.

"I know what happened to Sheena. She's a vampire." Climbing into the car, I looked to my friend. Frozen in the driver's seat, key halfway into the ignition, Norman's stare was unblinking. I worried that didn't hear me or didn't understand what I'd said so I repeated it. "Sheena's a vampire."

"Yeah," he gasped. "I heard you." Starting the engine, he managed to have one eye on the road and one remaining on me. I took his silence as a request for more.

Pulling the book from my pack, I flipped to the page that I'd marked. I didn't need to see it to know what was there; I'd read it enough times to commit it to memory. But I used the page nonetheless so he could see the source of the information. "The vampire can easily walk amongst humans unnoticed since they appear to the untrained eye to be mortal. In fact, looking closely reveals several tell-tale signs of their condition. The skin is flawless, showing no signs of aging or damage. The hair and nails are strong, without the damage that most adult humans are used to. The eyes are often a natural color but with a brightness that gives you pause. It isn't until the vampire's blood lust is triggered that one is able to see that they are not natural beings. This is when the fangs descend, and the eyes become entirely inhuman."

The sound of the book being slammed shut was the audible end to my revelation and I waited for my friend to have the same epiphany I didn't when I first read those words. Instead, he looked confused and a little worried about me. "I don't get it," he shook his head.

"Sheena," I exclaimed like it would give him clarity. "When she came to my window that night," I paused, certain he would now understand.

He didn't.

"Remember what she said and what happened. She said she'd come back for me and that she'd never be cold again. She said we'd see the world and be free. Then I cut myself. It was the blood, Norman. The blood is why she changed and ran away." I looked out the window but was oblivious to what we sped past. I was lost in the memory of the night she visited me. I could still see her face twisted in revulsion and fear, see her pulling back from me and running faster than anyone could run. "All these years of thinking my memories were messed up, that it couldn't have really happened that way." I turned to my friend, willing him to believe me. "But, it did. She didn't run away. She was turned into a vampire. I know it."

I let the silence hang in the car, waiting for his next thoughts so I would know what to say. "Okay," he finally broke. "Say that's real, that she's a vampire." He sucked in a deep breath and let it out. "How?"

Relief ran through my body like cool water. He believed me. "So, this book says that you have to have almost all your blood drained and then drink the vampire's blood. That's how you go from human to vampire."

"Okay," he coaxed. "So, if that's the case, if she's a vampire, good for her. I mean, she hasn't come back in all this time. Maybe she's in Montana, man. She's probably happy. Why would she ever come back here?"

"For me," I laughed. "She's going to come back for me. I was too young when she came to my window. She couldn't make me a vampire then so she's going to come when I'm old enough."

We pulled into our school parking spot, and he killed the engine. Rubbing his hands up and down this thigh, I knew he was nervous for whatever he was about to say. "But, Alex, you're older now than she was when she left. Wouldn't she have already come back?" I hadn't thought of that. I'd been so excited by the book and the idea that she was a vampire, I hadn't really dissected what it meant. His question had thrown me for a loop, and he wasn't done. "And," he continued. "Would you really want that? To live forever without the sun or food, drinking blood?"

He left me in the car to contemplate his question. If Sheena was a vampire and she did come back for me, is that what I wanted? I needed to know more before I landed on my decision. I'd only read the one book about vampires. How did I know this one was even accurate?

I couldn't get to the library fast enough. Dumping the other four books on the counter, I made my way to the card index and started to write down every book available on my desired subject. As each bell rang, marking the passing of the day, I didn't care that I'd missed every class. Nothing could have pulled me from my mission. Pages of scribbled information filled my notebook by the end of the last period, and I still had a stack to read. Choosing four of them to join the initial book wasn't easy but I knew I had access to the rest the next day.

My father was waiting for me when I walked through the door after school, which was not a good sign. I'd learned over the years to let him speak first so I could find out why he was mad and how bad it was about to get before I said something and possibly made it worse.

"You skipped school today?"

"No," I answered without thinking it through. The back of his hand cracked into my cheekbone, taking my vision away from me for a moment.

"Your school called and said you weren't in any of your classes so let's try this again. You skipped school today?"

I kept my eyes to the ground, knowing that he perceived direct eye contact as rebellion. "I was in the library," I asserted.

"Why weren't you in class?"

I couldn't tell the whole truth so I gave him the closest thing I could. "I have straight A's, sir. One day of missing classes won't change that. But I need to figure out what I'm majoring in, so I was in the library looking at options for what to study. It was my guidance counselor's idea." I fought the urge to look up. It meant I couldn't read his face, but I knew better than to search his eyes for whether or not he believed me. When he grabbed a handful of my hair and pulled my face up to meet his gaze, I couldn't stop my shaking. I hated that he felt me trembling and knew he loved it. What he didn't know what that my vibrating muscles were from a mix of fear and the overwhelming desire to start hitting him. Over his shoulder, I caught the sight of my mother, staring at the altercation and saying nothing.

"I'm calling your school and talking to the librarian *and* the counselor." Beer wafted off his breath and into my face. "If they don't back up your story, you're going to learn what real pain is." My mother turned and disappeared into the living room as he released my hair and shoved me back. Every fiber of my being tensed with the need to fight back. I knew my years of lifting meant I could hurt my tormentor, stop any further abuse by showing him what I was capable of, but I was frozen in place.

"Go to your room," he snapped. "You're pathetic. I'm disgusted just looking at you." He snatched a beer from the fridge. The crack of the can being opened and hiss of the gas being released were the soundtrack to my retreat into my room for the night. My stomach didn't growl until my parents were long asleep and it was safe to sneak leftovers. Another night came and went, lost to my voracious need to read every word I could from the books I'd smuggled into the house.

Norman didn't say a word as we rode to school, didn't call after me when I escaped his car and made a beeline for the guidance office. I didn't know every step I needed to take to reach my goal or if it was even possible, but I knew two things: I didn't want to be a vampire and I wanted to save Sheena from her current existence.

Mrs. Evans didn't bat an eye when I entered her office and told her what I'd decided.

"I want to be a doctor."

6

August 1996

The Last Day at Home

Norman loaded the last of my packed items into the back of his car. We wanted an early start the next morning since it was a full day's drive to my college, and we knew better than to think we'd get up an hour early to pack the car. Mr. Crawford gave him gas money and wished me luck in my endeavor. We talked about seeing each other at the holidays but I think he knew, just like I did, that I would never return to my childhood home. Mrs. Crawford was so blinded by her friendship with my mom that she refused to see the signs of my abuse. Her husband, on the other hand, showed me in a thousand different, quiet ways that he knew and felt bad for me. It was unspoken between us that he wanted to stop my father but knew that interfering would only make it worse for me. So, instead, he gave me extra helpings of food when I came over, let me sleep over on school nights, let me lift in their garage and slipped me a heavy envelope of cash as we said goodbye.

I wiped a single tear away from my eye when the father I wished I'd had disappeared into his house and didn't look back.

Norman and I agreed on a four am start then went into our respective homes to dread the inevitable moment when I stopped being his best friend across the street and started being the kid that never returned. It felt like walking through cement when I forced myself to take the steps to my front door and into the dining room. My parents sat in front of dinner like it was their last meals, scraping their utensils around their food but never bring it to their mouths. I joined the silent charade of eating until my father stood and left the room, signaling the end of the tableau. "I'll be up at 3:45 to make some coffee and then head out," I told my mother but could've been talking to an empty room for how unresponsive she was.

When my alarm sounded the next morning, I descended into a dark, empty kitchen. A can of Folgers sat on the counter, a mug next to it and the coffee maker filled with water. It was the closest thing to a heartfelt goodbye that I could expect. No one was going to cry as their baby boy left for college. Neither would thank me for earning a full scholarship or pat me on the back for going into the respected field of medicine. There would be no advice on how to navigate the new world of university or caution me away from fraternities. I'd been given an old mug from Goodwill and a can of coffee as my graduation gifts.

I left it all on the counter and decide to get coffee at a nearby 7-11. I didn't want anything from them and saw no need to even look back at the house as Norman reversed out of his driveway.

He'd been more than happy to take me for coffee, never asking how my last night with my parents went. He knew I'd tell him if I wanted to. Once the hot black liquid was in its white, green and orange Styrofoam cup with a donut as its companion, we were back on the road with no need to stop until our town was no more than a dot on a map.

"All right, tell me the plan one more time," he asked between gulps.

I listed off each step of my carefully crafted strategy. "Pre-med as quickly as I can. Then, I get into a med school with the best hematology program I can find."

"What's that again?" he interrupted.

"Blood, Spider. It's the medicine of blood." He nodded so I could keep going. "Once I know everything I can about blood, blood conditions and cures, I figure out what makes vampire blood change humans into vampires."

"And how do you do that?"

"Honestly, I don't know," I admitted. "That's what I'm hoping I learn in med school. Like one day I learn something that opens it all up, you know?"

"Okay," he was still following along. "But then what?"

"Well," this was the craziest part of the plan. "Once I know *how* vampires are made, then I figure out how to turn them back to human."

"Why?"

"So, I can find Sheena and cure her."

"But what if you don't find her or you do, and she doesn't want to be cured? Or what if you never figure it out?" He wasn't asking anything that I hadn't asked myself a million times. I tried to not get frustrated with his challenging but be grateful that he believed me.

"Then I'll still be a doctor and helping people," he nodded but it wasn't entirely true. The thought of not succeeding or of never finding Sheena was one I refused to accept. "I have to try, man. No one is looking for her. No one knows what she is or what she's going through. I'm her only hope."

He looked at me then back to the road. "Yeah, Alex. You're right. And if anyone can do this it's you. But, you gotta prepare yourself for the possibility that she doesn't want to be found. Maybe she's like living rich, in a castle in Transylvania and covered in jewels and happy."

"I hope you're right," I conceded. "But if you're not, if she's unhappy, I want to be able to offer her an alternative, you know?"

"I get it, man. I remember her. She was a cool chick. When the time comes, I want to help you find her."

I couldn't stop the smile that crossed my face just like I couldn't help the words that came out of my mouth. "Yeah. I'm sure that liberal arts degree is gonna be really helpful."

He scoffed. "I told you, that's not forever. I just need to figure out what my thing is. I'll switch to a real major when I know. Not all of us figured out our whole life already like Saint Alex."

Even though I hated that he'd been calling me that, I have to admit he was right. I'd found a purpose by accident. Not everyone had been that lucky. Most of our class wasn't even going to college. They'd gotten jobs with their parents or at local businesses, or gotten pregnant and married or told everyone they just needed a "gap year." Norman and I were one of the few who were headed to higher education and had a realistic shot at a future. I shouldn't give him a hard time for not knowing his major yet. As long as he was going to school, I should support him.

"You're right," I lifted my arms in surrender. "When do you start?"

"I'll move into the dorm in ten days. I totally get why you wanted to move in the second you were allowed but I'm not ready to leave my mom's cooking yet."

"I do get that. I will miss her lasagna, dude."

"They love you more than me. I bet my dad would drive it to you monthly if you asked." I don't think he was joking at all.

"Tempting," I chuckled. "But I wouldn't ask your mom to do that. I know it would put her in a weird place with my mom, having to choose between me and her best friend. I won't make her." Silence fell over the conversation. I regretted dampening the mood; I didn't want to talk about my parents anymore or ever again to be honest. "What are you most looking forward to in college?"

He perked up. "That's easy, the girls. They don't know me so I can reinvent myself. I'm not Spider, the weird lanky skateboard kid. I'm

Spider, the cool guy that's nice to girls, can shred a half-pipe and knows what to do in bed." He waggled his eyebrows.

"You had sex once," I reminded him. "That doesn't make you an expert."

"Ask Summer, my jealous friend. She said I was the best she's ever had."

"You're the only she's ever had," I watched disbelief cross his face. I used air quotes to make it clear that what I was about to tell him was fact and not my own words. "I hate to be the bearer of bad news but she got very drunk at Jason's grad party and was asking every guy there to be her 'second' so she could know if what you did is 'what it's always like'. I think she even approached a few girls."

"You lie," he gasped.

"I don't." I watched the gears churning in his brain as he tried to process what I'd just revealed. I took advantage of the quiet to look out the window. I watched the scenery I was so used to melt away into land I'd never seen before.

It was truly a fresh start for me, a new chapter. I couldn't get rid of the scars; they'd always remind me that the first 18 years of my life had been as bad as they were. But I knew, over time, the events I didn't want to keep in my brain could fade and disappear. No one controlled my mind but me. If I wanted to, I could choose to only keep the memories of my sister and my best friend, letting the rest go.

As my university got closer and closer, I felt like a man freed from a prison sentence he didn't earn. In four years, I'd be in medical school soaking up all the information I could until I was ready to save anyone cursed with the virus of vampirism. Once I knew how to cure her, I'd stop at nothing to find my sister.

For the millionth time, I wondered where she was and what her life was like. She simultaneously felt so far away and yet so close.

7

The first week of university was a whirlwind of orientation classes, meet and greets, getting lost on campus, learning what was palatable in the cafeteria and realizing that there was no such thing as quiet time in a dorm building. My roommate didn't show up until two days before classes started. I'd been at the campus gym, trying to establish a workout routine before my schedule became chaotic. When I'd returned to my room, band posters covered the once-sparse wall that the now-made bed was up against. No one was there to claim ownership, but I knew he couldn't be far since I'd only been gone for 90 minutes. It wasn't until I was showered and dressed that the boy I'd shared the room with made an appearance.

I could hear the music from his headphones before he opened the door and bounced in. The discman was tossed to the bed, causing whatever was playing to certainly skip. Brown hair fell in waves to his flannel-clad shoulders, pulled back from his cheery face by a cloth headband that I'd thought was just for girls until that moment. The orange Converse shoes that peeked out from jeans that were at least a size too big, were well-worn and scuffed. He reached out a hand. "I'm Isaac. Guess we're roomies. You like music?"

Reaching for his warm palm, he pumped my hand once and let it go, waiting expectantly for an answer. "Sure, I like music. I'm Alex."

"Cool," he beamed, nodding his head up and down like he was moving to a tune that only he could hear. "What kind?"

"Um," I felt nervous to answer. I didn't really know a lot about music and desperately wanted to have an easy relationship with him. I worried he may smell my lack of musical knowledge so spurted out my only thought. "Aerosmith."

"Nice choice, dude."

I breathed a sigh of relief. "My sister got me my first cassette when I was eight. I listened to it until it stopped working." Immediately I wished I'd not shared that and would definitely not tell him that the Walkman and cassette were in a shoebox under my bed. It was too lame.

"Cool beans, Alex. Tunes are more than the sounds, right? It's about the memories around them. That's why I'm a music therapy major. I want to help people that are traumatized with the healing power of music." His smile was warm and genuine. I knew my parents would hate him, immediately calling him a hippie and chastising his parentage while never getting to know Isaac or his family.

It made me like him.

"What about you?" He asked and it took me a second to understand what he was asking.

"Oh," I laughed. "Pre-med."

"Whoa," Isaac sighed. "Heavy."

"I guess," I conceded. "But, it's the same thing as you. I want to help people, just with medicine instead of music."

"Yeah," he continued to bounce his head to that inaudible rhythm. "Right on. That's cool. We're gonna get along just fine, man. But, first, I gotta nap." He threw himself backwards in a graceful arc that landed him in the center of his bed, laid back, crossed his feet, pulled the headphones back on, closed his eyes and rested his hands on his abdomen. He was instantly relaxed and lost in whatever song pumped into his eardrums. I envied this guy's ability to be so comfortable.

While he slept, I pulled out my journal and began to write about my first college week. Before meeting him, I had worried that my new roommate would think less of a male who scribbled in a book about his feelings. But after that brief encounter, I felt confident that Isaac likely didn't judge people harshly. As I wrote I reminded myself to call Norman. I hadn't talked to him since he'd dropped me off, helped me unpack and left the next morning to head home. I didn't know how to reach him once he went off to school. I needed to call and give him my dorm's telephone number before it was too late.

When Isaac woke, we decided on the rest of our day. We'd go get lunch in the cafeteria then find each one of our classrooms before the semester began, giving us an idea of the time we'd need to get to lectures. We ended up having one history class and one college writing class in common. Finding every room on our schedules had taken up the rest of the day and half of the next. Calling Norman had slipped my mind. It wasn't until I was rushing around on the first day of class that I realized I'd missed his departure to school. I told myself that he'd be so busy his first few months, he'd understand and forgive my lack of communication. I'd call him at his parent's house on his holiday break, and we'd catch up then. I wrote a reminder on my calendar for Christmas day then moved onto the rest of my schedule.

You know how sometimes you can look back on events and see the second your whole life goes into a new direction? It doesn't feel significant in the moment, but hindsight reveals that this one particular minute shifted everything.

One of those seismic shifts, for me, was walking into the last class of the day and seeing Hazel.

8

Intro to sociology was in one of the older buildings, in a room that desperately needed an update. The buzz of the overhead lights was the soundtrack to my entrance into the class I dreaded the most. It wasn't knowing I could easily pass the class that made me not want to take it. I just didn't see the point of taking a class that wouldn't help me reach my goal of being a doctor and saving my sister. I didn't see the need for me to take a social science. I wanted to jump straight to lectures on anatomy and how the body worked so I could feel like I was getting closer to my goal. To me, this class was time taken away from my purpose. I believed there would be nothing in this room that would make a difference.

Then, I saw the girl in the last row.

Her head was down as she scribbled away in a tattered notebook. At first, I thought she shared my habit of journaling. However, when she shifted enough for me to see her endeavor, I saw a pencil drawing of a young girl looking out a window. Scanning the room, I saw her muse. A quiet co-ed, that shared the likeness of the sketch, gazed out the classroom window while waiting for our professor to arrive. When I returned my gaze to the artist in the back, I saw she'd stopped her work in progress to look at me instead. I smiled, embarrassed that we'd locked eyes, but her warm smile showed me I was welcome at her table. As I approached, she pulled out the chair next to her as an unspoken agreement that I could join her.

"Hi." Her voice was unexpected. It held an aged quality to it, sounding older than her obvious years. "I'm Hazel."

"Hi. Alex." I answered as I took the offered seat. Pulling out the required text and a fresh notebook, I zipped up my bag and tossed it to the floor.

When she returned to her drawing, I used the time to really look at her. Her brown hair was a stark contrast to her pale skin. Chestnut smears along her hairline told me she'd colored it the night before or that very morning. Several slender braids were scattered throughout the curls with a feather clipped to one side. A number of necklaces decorated the front of her long-sleeved raven blouse at varying lengths and bracelets fought for space on each slender wrist. I was thinking about how the silver and gold chains, colorful bracelets and white feather stood out nicely against the black outfit and dark hair, then I saw her eyes. They were a startling green that shone out from her coal lined lids. To say I was attracted would be the wrong choice of words; I was intrigued. I somehow knew this girl had an interesting story to tell and I wanted to hear it.

"What's your major?" She asked. I gotten used to this question. Seemed like every person I encountered wanted to know. I was liking walking into a prison and being asked what you were in for.

"Pre-med," I answered. "You?"

"Sociology," she winked.

"Oh, good. You can help me pass this class then." This got a laugh from her, and the joyful sound was so odd coming out of someone that dressed like she was going to a funeral. "What?" I asked.

She flipped the page she was drawing on to an unused one and set it down for later use. "Anyone who is smart enough to become a doctor doesn't need help with this class."

"I thank you for the vote of confidence, but you don't know that. I may be utterly helpless."

She arched an eyebrow. "I somehow doubt that."

"So, why Sociology?"

"I don't know," she smiled. "I needed a major and didn't want something super hard but also don't want to waste time. I guess I want to understand people and why they do what they do, you know?"

"Sure, but what can you do with a sociology degree?" I hoped it didn't sound condescending. It must not have because she answered.

"You can teach it, or you can take it into grad school and go into like counseling. Why be a doctor?" She seemed genuinely interested.

"To help people," I responded.

"So," she punched my arm. "Not to be rich and marry a model and drive a Mercedes?"

That made me laugh. To be honest, I'd never even considered that my career would bring me money, but I couldn't tell her that. How would I explain that my ultimate goal was to cure my vampire sister? She'd think I was insane. So, I just shrugged mischievously and let her believe that the wealth was my true motive.

Before we could finish our discussion, an older man with a briefcase came into the room and took his place at the front. The snaps of his case being opened echoed through the space. He had a "no-nonsense" air about him, commanding silence just by his entrance. When he wrote DR. FLYNN - SOC 101 across the board, the chalk cracked from the force of his sharp letters. I knew this was going to be far from an easy A.

Dr. Flynn fit a lot into his allotted 90 minutes. I struggled to stay on pace with his lecture, frantically trying to follow along in the text while taking notes. His syllabus made it clear that he took his subject seriously and expected his students too as well. He proudly stated that half of the people in the room would likely drop his lecture as soon as they walked out that evening, the rest would either keep up or fail out. Hazel didn't write anything down, just stared at the man like she was memorizing every word that came out of his mouth. Every once in a while, she'd highlight something in the text, but she appeared to already know the content well enough to not sweat the inevitable exam on the material. Meanwhile, two students just got up and walked out halfway in. By the time he excused everyone for the night, a quarter of my spiral notebook was full and the girl who'd been staring out the window earlier, left in tears.

"I don't know about you," Hazel let out a sigh. "But I'm starved. Dinner?"

"Sure," I agreed. We both stood and gathered our things. I followed behind her, inwardly begging myself to act cool and not make it obvious that I'd never had a meal with a girl before.

I felt a mixture of relief and disappointment when we entered the student cafeteria and saw Isaac. I was relieved because I knew his relaxed vibe would make conversation easy. I was disappointed because part of me wanted Hazel all to myself. Isaac waved at me and made a gesture to show that the rest of the table was open. Crossing to him, I made the introductions. "Isaac, this is Hazel. Hazel, this is my roommate Isaac." She laid her bag across an empty chair and stuck out her hand, he took it and gave it a pump. "We're gonna grab food and we'll be back." I explained.

"Right on," he beamed and plopped down to start on his heaping plate.

Ten minutes later, the three of us began to discuss our first day of college. Hazel and I had chosen to take advantage of the surprisingly impressive salad bar. The only difference between our two creations was that I'd placed cold, grilled chicken on top the vegetables and she hadn't. She'd used that opportunity to explain she was a vegetarian, and I'd explained that I would never give up meat. Our dinners were colorful when contrasted with Isaac's plate. He'd mixed several hot foods together into a type of buffet casserole. Chicken tenders, macaroni and cheese, French fries and something that may have been a marinara pasta dish were all piled on top of each other, and he scooped spoonfuls of the concoction into his mouth with zeal.

"I think the hardest part for me," Isaac said around one of his smaller bites. "Will be making sure I have enough time to still practice."

"Practice what?" Hazel asked.

"Oh," he swallowed with effort and wiped his mouth. "Music. I play the guitar, so I want to keep up with that, but I also signed up for piano lessons, so I need to reserve one of the practice rooms now before they're full, but I don't totally know my schedule yet. Like, I need a week to figure it all out to know what day and time I'll be most likely to play but, in a week, the rooms may all be reserved, you know?"

She thought for a moment and then held up a finger like she'd just solved a difficult equation. "So, go reserve a day and time now for the rest of the semester, one you think might work. Then, if it turns out there would be a better day and time, and it's taken, find the person who took it and offer a trade for the one you signed up for."

Isaac and I exchanged looks. "Actually," he clapped. "That's a pretty good idea."

The smile he gave her was warm and reached his eyes. I saw the change in the way he looked at her and hoped it was all in my head. She smiled back the same way, holding his gaze. "And when you pick that day and time," she touched the top of his hand. "Let me know cuz I'd love to come hear you play."

And, I knew my window of opportunity with Hazel had just closed and been nailed shut.

9

The three of us became inseparable. Isaac quickly became one of my favorite people. He seemed to exude joy and made you want to be around him. Everywhere we went, fellow students would be drawn to him and then leave us with smiles on their faces just from talking to Isaac. His laugh was full, like it came from his chest. He never judged and was giving of his time, heart and genuine advice. He knew more about music than anyone I'd ever met, played more instruments than I knew existed. Hazel was a ball of energy and light. She didn't trust people easily but was utterly herself around Isaac and I. She talked about stars and moon cycles in a way that always reminded me of Sheena, which didn't make me sad like I thought it would. Instead, it gave me a type of peace, knowing that there were other girls like my sister who had happy lives.

Monday through Friday, I'd get up, hit the gym early, shower and wake up Isaac. Then we'd head to the cafeteria and meet up with Hazel for breakfast. We'd split off to go to our classes and meet up at the end of each day for dinner.

Saturdays were for hanging out. After breakfast, Hazel would come back to our dorm room for TV or listening to music or talking about what our lives were like before school and what we hoped they'd be like in the future. During the latter activity, I'd just listen. Whenever pushed for personal information, I'd make something up. Sometimes I'd tell stories from Norman's house, just letting my friends assume that was my family. I never talked about my parents or Sheena; I didn't want the way they looked at me to show a hint of pity. So, I'd give a brief tidbit of information and then ask a question to return to the topic to one of them.

Sundays were for serious studying. We'd meet up at the campus library and spend most of the day in quiet schoolwork and scholarly pursuits. From 1:00-3p, I'd be alone while Hazel went to listen to Isaac play whatever instrument he was mastering. Her idea had panned out perfectly for him. He'd initially reserved every Thursday at 5pm but didn't want to miss dinner with Hazel and I. When he'd approached the student who'd reserved the Sunday slot, she'd been thrilled to trade since it meant she could go home every weekend. I'd learned quickly that Isaac could pick up almost any piece of musical equipment and be proficient on it in no time. Hazel was obviously enamored with him, but it'd taken him almost a month and a half to finally ask her out.

By the end of the second month of the semester, she'd started staying over some nights, curled up in his twin bed with him. That was something I needed time to get used it. It wasn't that I was jealous; I'd genuinely started caring about her as a friend and was happy for them. It's just that "third wheel" feeling made me cringe. I'd hear them whispering and giggling and I thought I should give them privacy but didn't have any other friends on campus, so nowhere to go. So, those nights, I just laid there in the dark, on my side, facing the wall, and tried to sleep.

It was Thanksgiving week when Hazel came to us and told us she'd joined a fantasy group that met three times a week at 9pm so she wouldn't be hanging out those nights. We didn't ask any questions; the sparkling in her eyes told us that she was ecstatic, and we didn't have ownership over her time, so we told her to have fun. We could see her the other nights.

"What do you think it is?" Isaac asked when she'd laid a kiss on his check and skipped out of the cafeteria to go get ready for her first meeting.

"D&D?" I guessed.

"Maybe," he answered. "I know she's been getting into Wicca. Maybe it's something to do with that."

"Possible," I agreed. "There's so many damn clubs and groups; it could literally be anything."

"So true," he laughed.

Honestly, I was happy for a few nights of just us guys and earlier bedtimes. Isaac was so focused on Hazel that I worried he was losing study time. He was a grown up and could do whatever he wanted but if he failed out of school, I'd lose a great roommate and friend. Selfish, I know. But it's what I was thinking.

"I'm sure she'll tell us all about it tomorrow," he shrugged. "Unless it's some kind of secret society, in which case, I probably don't want to know."

"Good call." We picked up our trays and disposed of everything. The air was crisp, and I wished I chosen something heavier than a t-shirt as the sun set. Huddling against the cold, we powerwalked back to the dorm.

"Going home for turkey?" I asked.

"Nah," his voice quivered, and I knew he was just as cold. "It's too quick of a turn around. I'll go home for winter break. You?"

"Nah," I answered. "I'll stay here for both. I have so much to do." I knew that excuse would explain my missing Thanksgiving but was not a good enough reason to stay on campus for our month off between the two semesters. "And, my parents are going oversees this Christmas, so I'd just be in an empty house." As soon as it was out, I worried it was too wild of a lie. Do people go to Europe for a whole month?

We rushed into our building and shut the door to the cold. Thankfully the thermostat was cranked up in the dorms and we were hit with a wall of heat. "Oh man," Isaac said. "Dude, that sucks. Come home with me for the holidays. It's gonna be so depressing here all alone."

I lead the way to our room and trusted that he followed. I didn't want him to see my face as I tried to work out a way to get out of this web of untruths without hurting his feelings or raising suspicions. "That's so nice, Isaac. I don't think so, though. I really need the down time. I'm looking forward to nothing but gym time, reading and going on walks. I'm going to call my friend Norman a bunch too, catch up with him."

Isaac slapped my back. "All right, Alex. But, if you change your mind, just call. I'm only a four-hour train ride away and you're welcome anytime. I'll even give you the top bunk."

I laughed. The offer was so kind, and I knew Isaac meant every word of it. I had to imagine the family that created this sweet soul was just as warm. So why didn't I take his offer and finally experience a happy family holiday? Because deep down I worried that they'd see the brokenness in me, like being surrounded by that type for normalcy would shine a spotlight on my hidden scars. So, I nodded like I may consider his invitation but knew I wouldn't.

I'd stay on this campus with the other unwanted things and silently be thankful that being alone was 100 times better than what I came from. And, not going home was my Christmas gift to myself.

The next morning, we saw Hazel at breakfast. Lack of sleep had darkened her eyes, and she did more playing with her oatmeal than eating. Isaac kissed the top of her head and dropped into the seat next to her. "Long night?" he asked.

"Yeah," she sighed. "It was done by midnight but we all stayed and talked until almost four." Pushing her bowl away, she lowered her forehead to the table. "I have regrets."

"Miss classes," he rubbed her back. "Go sleep."

"I can take notes for you in soc. Will you miss anything important in the other ones?" I asked.

She looked up to think about it. "Exams in the first two."

"So," I counseled. "I'll grab you some coffee. Get those two exams done and skip the rest. Go sleep. Doctor's orders."

She smirked. "Yeah. I mean today's the last day til next Tuesday anyways. Everyone's going home tomorrow for Thanksgiving." She slapped the tabletop with both palms. "Go get that caffeine, Alex. I can do this."

As I headed for the coffee, I heard Isaac ask her about the group. I didn't hear all of the response but knew she'd said she was too tired and would tell us all about it when she'd slept.

She didn't, though. She slept through dinner and through that night. Then, left the next day for the holiday weekend at home. When she returned the following week, she'd stopped by the dorm to say hi, give Isaac a kiss and then told us she was headed to "the club" for a meeting.

The two weeks post-Thanksgiving were a whirlwind of lectures for finals, studying for finals and then actual finals. The last day of the semester we heard the sounds of celebrating throughout campus. Dr. Flynn's predictions had been accurate; only half the initial class had made it to the end and according to the posted final grades only 25% of us has passed.

Hazel and I were one of the lucky few to never have to retake that class.

In the middle of the courtyard, someone had set up a massive burn barrel. Flames were leaping from it as students threw notebooks and handouts into the fire. Hazel and I tossed our Sociology notes into the pyre and danced around it like it was some kind of ritual cleansing. We spun around the barrel and cried out in joy. Several students joined us in our revelry. To anyone watching, we must've looked like witches on a full moon, casting spells and twirling around flames. Mid-spin, she stopped and grabbed my arms. In the midst of her hyperventilation, she asked, "Are you staying for winter break?"

"Yeah, why?"

"Because," she leaned in so she could whisper. "I want to bring you to the group."

We waved goodbye to Isaac as the train pulled away. I didn't like that Hazel hadn't invited Isaac to this club that she'd obviously grown fond of and that we didn't tell him I would be going. It felt too much like hiding a secret from a friend, too much like a betrayal. But simultaneously, I was excited to spend time with just Hazel. Over the months, she'd become so important to me. I didn't totally see it at the time, but she was so similar to Sheena, it was almost like having my sister back. The two girls shared the same wild spirit and unfettered love of life. They both had this infectious way of spreading their joy so that their sheer presence took worry and doubt away. In a way, watching Hazel experience college and talk about the dreams of her future was like seeing what Sheena would have gotten if her life had gone differently.

I loved Hazel like my sister and because I didn't see her romantically, it felt like the secret we kept from Isaac was okay. I told myself that I would convince Hazel to share her group with him too once he was back but, for now, it would just be for us.

We were seated in a booth at a local diner and had just ordered lunch when I finally pushed her to tell me what I was getting myself into. "Okay, Hazel, it's time to fess up. What's this group I'm going to tonight? Do they know I'm coming? And is anyone even still here?"

"Normally there's like 12 of us but I think 5 or 6 people went home for break. The rest, though, they're like us. We'd rather die than go back." She stared at me, waiting for my reaction. I took a second to process what those words meant.

"How?" I swallowed hard and sipped at water to buy myself some time. "I mean, what do you mean?"

She laid her hand on mine and waited for me to move my eyes to hers. "You don't have to tell me, it doesn't matter. And, if you're like me, you're trying to forget it all anyways." She rolled her hand over, palm up on the table, then pulled up her sleeve to show me the scars that crisscrossed over that porcelain skin. "Now, because of where mine are, it's hard to know that they're not my own work." She pulled the sleeve back down. "But I've seen yours. No one scars their own back."

Tears threatened to escape, and I didn't want her to see but I couldn't look away. I wanted so badly to be the normal, well-adjusted person that I presented to everyone, but she'd seen right through it. I reminded myself that she must know because she'd come from the same thing, not because I didn't play the part well. It was a sort of devastating comfort. Until that moment, it never occurred to me that other people came from abuse. The realization that Hazel could have endured the same childhood I did washed over me. She'd hid it so well in all her stories, never even hinted at abuse. But the scars didn't lie.

"I-" Words failed me. Before I could overthink it, I went with honesty. "I'll never go back."

"You'll like the people in this group, Alex. They're like us. They came from shit and found something that makes them happy. It makes me happy. And, I want to share it with you."

"So, what is it? Like a therapy thing?" I really didn't want to be in some group where everyone sat in a circle of metal chairs talking about their crappy parents. I was working on a way to get out of it without hurting her feelings.

Her laugh was full and warm, pulling a smile from me. "No. Nothing like that." Our food arrived, postponing the big secret for a few minutes while she squirt ketchup onto her fries and I cut my steak into small bites. "Have you ever heard of LARP?"

Swallowing my mouthful of meat, I washed it down with water and shook my head.

"Well," she looked up, searching for the words. "Think of it like a fantasy improv theater troupe." I started to protest and she held up her hands to silence me. "Wait, let me explain." I nodded, agreeing to listen but already wanting to skip the night's activity.

"Each of us has chosen a character type. Then you pick a name. You get powers. And you all interact as these characters. People wear costumes and contacts and makeup. Like, everyone really gets into it. Then the story teller or master for the night, has this storyline that he throws out and we all react as our characters."

"D&D?" So, Isaac and I had guessed accurately in the beginning.

She shook her head. "Kind of but no. You see, Dungeons and Dragons is on a table top. We're out, in the campus, actually playing it and acting it out. LARP stands for live action role playing."

"Okay," I wasn't following yet. "And, why did you think I would like it? No offense, but what made you decide to invite me?"

She laid down her silverware, her stare showing me she was very serious. "Haven't you ever wanted to escape for a few hours? Be someone else? Someone powerful and strong? Someone who would never be a victim or who turned their tragic backstory into something wonderful?"

"Yes," it was out before I even knew I was thinking it.

"This is a way to do that," she smiled. "Everyone there wants the same thing. We all play along and get to just be different people in a beautiful world for a few hours."

"So, what do I need to do?" I still couldn't imagine myself running around the grounds acting like a wizard, but I was intrigued enough to ask for the next step.

"They all know you're coming tonight. You have to ask the whole group if a new person wants to join and they're all cool with it. So, we just need to come up with a character for you then introduce it tonight. The master said tonight will be an easy story so you can just watch or join in, whatever you want."

The waitress asked us if we wanted dessert. I normally didn't indulge but that day somehow felt special so we each ordered an ice cream sundae. I took the time between her taking our plates and bringing the treat to process everything Hazel had told me. I'd always been an introvert. The idea of going to a group of new people was already overwhelming but add in role playing and I was way out of my comfort zone. I didn't think I could do it. But, looking into her eyes, I couldn't help but think of Sheena. I knew my sister would have loved something like this. She would have already been on her way to a thrift shop for a costume.

"What kind of characters are there?"

Her smile widened. I think, until that moment, she hadn't been sure if I'd join. Something about that question told her that I'd join that night. It seemed to really please her, which made me happy. "There's this book in my dorm. It tells you all the basics of the game and all the types of characters. We'll start with the blood line you want and then build from there. We still have time to put together a really cool character, find some clothes for you and maybe even get a nap."

"Whoa," I held up my hands. "I agreed to ask questions, not wear whatever you have in mind."

"Come on, Alex. Trust me. With that bod, the right outfit could send some of the girls into convulsions. You'll be fighting them off."

I busied myself with scraping the last of the chocolate syrup from the bottom of the sundae glass. Intellectually, I knew that Hazel meant that as a compliment. But the tightness in my chest was a reflex. Outside of my one embarrassing fumble with Nancy in a closet, I hadn't been with anyone else or even thought about sex. I was so focused on my education and my goal to find Sheena that it hadn't really occurred to me that I could have a bunch of unattached liaisons like most of the other students. College was about exploration and finding yourself, right? Was I missing out by not having a different girl in my bed as often as I'd like to?

I cleared my throat. "Let's start slow, okay? Tell me about the game and we'll go from there."

She raised her hand in the air "Check, please," she shouted to our frazzled server.

Ten minutes later, we were walking back to the dorm. She was talking fast and I was struggling to keep up with her words as she struggled to keep up with my long stride. "They're going to love you, Alex. And, I really hope you like this. I mean, it's okay if you don't but I really hope you do. I am obsessed with the game. I mean, I'm still one of the weaker ones in the group but I'm working my way up."

Entering her hall, we were met with the silence of a mostly empty building. I hadn't ever been into her room and suddenly felt uncomfortable with the idea of going into the place she slept with my friend's girlfriend. I reminded myself that we weren't doing anything wrong; we were friends and nothing else. Her door had two black pieces of paper with red writing that declared HAZEL and IRIS lived in this room. Perfume filled the air when she swung the door open to reveal the mystery that is a girls' dorm room.

Christmas lights danced around the ceiling, being run across the top from side to side in a zig-zag. Construction paper flowers were stuck all over the walls, instantly making me think of the book *A Secret Garden*, one of the few stories that had made me cry as a boy. A book shelf sat between the two twin beds, filled with well-worn paperbacks. "Wow," I sighed.

"Yeah," she beamed. "My first roommate and I didn't get along. I met Iris in the LARP, and we requested a trade. Cindy left and Iris moved in. Both were very happy about it."

She threw her bag onto her bed and dropped to her knees, pulling out something from under it. Sitting on her bed, she patted the space next to her. "So, I'll read you the intro and then the traits of each blood line. You pick the one you like the most, then we go from there. Cool?"

Again, I had the sensation that I shouldn't be here, in a dorm room, about to sit on a bed with Isaac's girlfriend when he was miles away. But I shoved it to the back of my mind. My curiosity was too strong, and I had to know what this book held.

Sitting on the bed, Hazel flipped the book so I could see what all the fuss was about. My breath caught in my chest and the world swam around me.

Across the front, in bold lettering, I read **Raven Realm: Vampires**

"**Y**ou okay, Alex? You look like you've seen a ghost."

Not a ghost, I thought. *Vampires.* But I didn't say it out loud. Instead, I said "This is a vampire thing?"

"Yeah," she cracks open the book. "Isn't it cool? So, in this world, you can be all kinds of different fantasy creatures. Almost everyone in the group is a vampire, but I'm a witch and Iris is a fairy so you can pick something different if you want. Raven Realm is a whole universe and there are different games with different species. This one just happens to be vampires."

"Why vampires?" I couldn't just straight out ask her if she thought they were real, let alone trauma dump on her that I did think they were real and that my sister was one and my whole major was based on this belief.

"I don't know," she shrugged. "I mean, who wouldn't want to be a vampire? They're young forever and strong and have magical powers."

"What if they don't? I mean, what if you become a vampire and don't want to be one?"

Confusion crossed her face. "But you don't have to. I just said you can pick whatever you want. Just so long as it's in the book. Honestly, though, I bet they'd let you pick whatever as long as you have a good idea of your abilities, weaknesses and all that." She flipped through the book, looking for a specific page. "Just pick wisely because you're going to have to stick with it and you don't want any regrets. Do you want to be a vampire?"

So, she doesn't think they're real. I let out a breath and tried to hide my swirling thoughts. "Um, so what kind of vampires are there?"

Laying the book in my lap, it was opened to the page she'd been seeking. The word *Bloodlines* was scrawled across the top in Edwardian script. Below it, in two columns, a list of names was then described by traits. I read over each one slowly, trying to take in every word while also trying to calm my racing heart. "You can pick a line that's totally different than you or one that's the person you want to be or one that's the most like you, it's whatever you want."

What type of man did I want to be in this game? Would I even go tonight, let alone more than once? Was this a futile exercise? All I knew is that I couldn't let Hazel down. She was so excited and me backing out now might do damage to our friendship that I couldn't repair.

One description sent a shiver over my body, followed by a flushing of heat. *A bloodline of warriors, protectors of the realm. Usually trained from a young age and turned once they are strong enough to use their skills, vampires from this line fight for those who can't fight. Their mission is to rid the realm of anyone from the Dark Provence who seeks to destroy the realm and take power. Their strengths include battle strategy, weapons knowledge, survival knowledge, fortitude and might. Weaknesses include difficulty in love, lack of charisma and inability to masquerade.* I pointed at this section. "What's masquerade?"

"Oh, that's like being able to hide in plain sight. Because that bloodline is big and strong, they tend to stick out like a sore thumb. The Enkil line is perfect for you. You're already all muscle and like 7 feet tall. Plus, no one else has chosen that line."

"I'll take it, then. Make me Enkil."

She jumped up and clapped her hands. "Yay! Okay," she bounced. "So, what is your character's name?"

"Uh, I don't know. I'm not creative. You pick." I was fighting back the urge to run from the room and never look back.

"Alright," she paced around. "Something heroic like Hercules but not that lame." Inspiration hit her and she grabbed a book from the shelf, flipping through, tossing it aside and grabbing another one. "I got it," she squealed. "Ajax."

"Ajax?" I questioned.

"Yeah. Big, strong, a great warrior. Ajax, you know? From the Iliad? He was, like, the best fighter and when his cousin dies, he rescues the body. I mean, he ends up going mad and killing himself, but his blood makes this beautiful red flower. Cool, right? Plus, it's close to Alex so it's easy to remember."

"Ajax." I let the name soak in. Was I really going to do this? Looking into her hopeful eyes, I knew I was. "I love it."

"Yes," she celebrated. "So, what kind of look do you want? I mean, what is your back story?"

"Um, I'm not sure I know what you mean." Regret was already slinking into my thoughts.

She grabbed a notebook and a pencil, then sat next to me again. "Like, where did Ajax come from? How old is he?"

"You pick," I relented.

"How about this?" she started to scribble some things down. "Ajax was born to a poor farming family. They couldn't afford all the children, so they sold Ajax into the realm's army."

"Wait," she was annoyed that I paused her, but I had so many questions. "There's humans?"

"Yeah," she sighed. "Sorry. I need to go back. So, in the Raven Realm there are humans. But there are also all these other magical creatures. The vampires are in charge, like royalty and everyone knows it, and everyone gets along. And, there is also the Dark Provence.

This is just outside of the Realm. In the Dark Provence are all the bad creatures. So, like, the bad vampires and humans and fairies and witches who want to take over the Raven Realm for themselves." I nodded and she returned to writing out Ajax's tragic history. "So, the army is using Ajax as like a stable boy but as he grows, they see how big and strong he's getting. So, they start to train him. And, when he's grown, we'll say like 22, they embrace him into the Enkil bloodline to be a warrior with them."

"Embrace?"

"Yeah," she didn't look up. "When you get made into a vampire. You know? They drink from you, and you drink from them."

So that part of the game lined up with what I'd researched. Did that mean that part was real? It was hard to tell with all the fantasy around it, but it did send a thrill through me. Maybe joining this group would actually help me learn about vampires? But even as I thought it, I knew it was a stretch. I was just trying to convince myself that doing this wasn't a waste of time and very stupid.

"Ajax has been with the Enkil Army for 100 years. Do you like that? I mean, it's not that long in the vampire world but it's enough to have learn some things. So, you'd be one of the youngest warriors. Is that okay?"

"Sounds good to me."

"This is just the beginning, too. As you continue in the game, you'll create more about your character and your story, but this is a good start." While she'd been talking and I'd been thinking, I was assuming she'd been writing down a story for me, like lecture notes, but I'd been wrong. When she lifted up the notebook to show me, I saw that she'd been sketching me. Well, not me, but the Ajax version of me. My face was the same, put she'd made my hair a little longer. My arms were bare in the vest she'd put on me and a sword protruded from behind my head. While she'd made my shoulders and biceps much larger than reality, she'd also added my very accurate scars. When I met her eyes, kindness looked back. "He has battle scars, scars from a war he was forced into by circumstance and the need to survive. He has scars from protecting those who can't fight like he can."

And that was it; that was the moment that I gave into the game and Hazel fully became the sister I'd needed for so long.

"You don't have to show your arms if you don't want to," she tossed the notebook onto her roommate's bed. "But this is the group to do it in. No one will judge and you get to be the person who fights back, for once."

For the second time that day, I wrestled back emotions I didn't want to have. "Where am I supposed to find this outfit? I don't own anything like that."

She grabbed my hands and pleaded. "Please, let me get them. I'll measure you and go to the secondhand store. Please? I live for this, and I promise you won't regret it."

"Oh boy," I shook my head. "I'm already regretting it." But her measuring tape was out and she was pulling me up to wrap it around my waist before I could stop her.

12

I tried to nap while Hazel was on her mission to build Ajax's wardrobe. After an hour of tossing and turning, I headed to the gym instead. After pushing every one of my muscles to its breaking point and standing in a very hot shower, I had two hours to kill and was finally fatigued enough to doze off. It felt like only five minutes had gone by when I was awakened by Hazel's knocking.

Stumbling to the door in the dark and opening it meant I couldn't see her clearly at first. I had to adjust to the burst of hallway light. She was in and flipped on the light before my vision was fully back. Only then did I remember I was only in boxers.

We both just stared at each other.

She stood in front of me; her was hair piled on top in a mass of curls and braids. A single curl fell from the side, down to her shoulders and cascaded over her chest. The evergreen bodice hugged her tight and gave her the appearance of being more ample than she probably was. Around her shoulders and down to the floor, a vibrant purple cloak that matched her amethyst skirt, pooled down and shifted with her every movement. Glitter shimmered on her exposed arms, enhancing the scars but somehow making them part of her magic. Her eyes ran up and down my body, making me very aware of my state of undress.

"Oh, man. I'm so sorry. Let me get something on."

She stepped into me. "No, I'm sorry. I shouldn't stare. I've just never seen so many muscles." She held up a plastic bag and shoved it into my chest. "Here, I think they'll fit. I hope you like it. I'll step out into the hallway." She did as she said, shutting the door as she stepped out, then speaking from the other side. "Call if you need help."

The first out of the bag was a brown, suede vest. It reminded me of something a cowboy would wear. But, all over the material, brown leather patches had been sewn on, overlapping, almost like scales on a dragon. As I pulled it on and buttoned it up, the smell of warm leather hit my nose. I had to admit, it fit like it was made for me and made me feel strong. Next, from the bag, came brown leather pants that were a little too tight for my comfort. However, when I looked in the mirror, I had to admit I looked amazing. I was confused by the black belt since the pants had no belt loops. "Hazel?"

She stepped in and halted mid-step, whistling. "Damn, Alex. You look better than I imagined." Heat rose on my cheeks. I lifted the belt with a questioning look. "Oh," she smirked. "It goes loosely around your waist, like for a sword on your hip." She stepped in, taking the belt from me and fit it in place. Upon inspection in the mirror, she was right. I looked like some kind of knight in King Arthur's court.

"I'll have to grow my hair out to match your picture," I joked.

"It would be a shame to hide those eyes, but yeah. I think a little longer hair and you'd put Prince Charming to shame." She ran to the hallway. "Oh wait. You need these." Returning to my side, she held up black riding boots. I arched an eyebrow. "C'mon, Ajax. You trusted me with the rest, just try."

As I wrestled on the boots and struggle to zip them up over my calves, I asked. "How did you even find all this stuff?"

"Please," she scoffed. "I've spent my whole life picking through bargain bins and yard sales to put together a wardrobe that doesn't look like it comes from bargain bins and yard sales. Once, I sewed on the patches, it was utter perfection for $20 total."

"Let me pay you back," I insisted, even though my money from Mr. Crawford was dwindling by the day.

"No way," she answered. "It's my thank you gift for agreeing to do this. I really do think you'll like it."

Standing to face the mirror for the third time, I had to admit that Hazel was a genius. Even I couldn't argue with the fact that I looked like a warrior. My blue eyes radiated from within the brown and black ensemble. My chest swelled under the vest and my arms looked strong. I could halfway imagine myself, on horseback, rescuing princesses and slaying evil wizards.

"What's your name?" I turned to her. In all the excitement of building my new persona, I hadn't even thought to ask her about the character that she obviously loved.

She twirled and the cape billowed around her. "Morganna, but you can call me Mor." I bowed and she curtsied. "Ready?"

"As I'll ever be."

"It's actually a really nice night for December. You probably don't even need a coat."

Stepping out into the night, I saw that she was right. It was unseasonably warm and felt more like early autumn than winter. Stars exploded across the clear sky, sparkling around a full, bright moon. "I hope we play outside tonight," she squealed. "We might need to get you a cloak for January and February."

"Let's get through tonight and see if I decide to keep playing before Ajax gets anymore clothes," I chuckled.

"You're right," she relented. "No pressure. If you don't like it, that's totally fine. You can use the outfit for Halloween or something."

The walk was quicker than I expected. We entered into the rec building and turned right down a long hallway. Most of these rooms were for club meetings so it made sense that we'd start here for the night. The hint of coffee filled the air, but it was more like a ghost of the substance than the real thing. There had probably been so many pots made over in the years that the essence of it was in every pore of the walls and carpet. We stopped at a door, and she turned to me. "Ready?" She didn't wait for my answer, just pushed it open and stepped in.

Music played quietly in the corner, and I saw a small silver CD player. The song was some kind of new age thing and fit perfectly with what I was witnessing. A dozen people stood in smaller clumps, talking excitedly. Almost everybody was cloaked in a cape, and I was suddenly glad that I had let her dress me. If I'd arrived in jeans and a t-shirt, I would have felt very out of place. All eyes turned to us. A girl ran over and hugged Hazel. Her blond hair was pulled back, and I saw pointed ear pieces had been affixed to the top of both ears.

"This is Alex," Hazel said to the girl who had to be the fairy roommate. She was barely five feet so had to crane her neck to meet my eyes but first she let her eyes trail down and up my length. I fought to hide my embarrassment and tried to play the part of a brave, battle-hardened combatant.

"Hi," she beamed. "I've heard so much about you."

I took her hand and brought it to my lips, bowing. "My lady." The move that even shocked me; I worried it was too much. Still bowing, I looked up to see her response and was relieved that she not only didn't think it was too much but rolled with the bit.

"Warrior," she answered.

I lifted myself upright and dropped her hand as the others came to join us. Hazel started the introductions. Along with my friend and her roommate, ten more players had joined in that night. They were Tony, Marie, Lucy, Rachel, Chris, Julian, Melanie, Drew, Amanda and Heather. I realized quickly that Tony and Marie, as well as Amanda and Heather, were couples. Drew explained, right out of the gate, that he was the game master this year and came up with all the story lines. This was obviously a source of pride for him. Every member of the group welcomed me warmly, complemented my outfit and thanked me for joining. I didn't have the heart to tell them that I hadn't officially decided to join. I looked at each of them and was genuinely impressed by their commitment. I saw movie level makeup, costumes that rivaled Broadway and a few sets of contacts. Rachel's were a bright, blood red, Julian's were a sparkling, emerald green and Chris' were white. It was hard to even look him in the eyes because the contacts were so eerie. "Are those uncomfortable?" I asked.

"At first," he answered. "But you get used to it."

The group seemed thrilled that I'd chosen to be from the Enkil bloodline since they never had one. I secretly told myself to borrow Hazel's book and read up on the bloodlines again, so I didn't look as ignorant about them as I actually was.

I learned that the night would start with a description of the previous few sessions to catch up anyone who had missed and refresh the memories of those who were there. Then, when Drew called out *"in game"*, we'd all go into character and not drop them until the game master said. He took me aside to assure me he would explain how I was brought into the storyline and all I had to do was listen, then play when I was ready. I appreciated the help but was quickly becoming just as eager to play as the rest.

When we all stepped out into the night and I heard the words "In game," I understood why Hazel loved the club as much as she did. Each member stuck to their characters and the game completely. They slowly pulled me into the story in a way that made me feel safe and supported. I quickly grew fond of my warrior's mission to protect, saving a few of the girls that night from an evil sorcerer who was sent by the Dark Provence to capture them for ransom.

Three hours later, we'd finished our story for the night, and I was sad to say goodbye to Ajax. I'd quickly fallen into the world, becoming the fearless protector of the realm that Alex had always wished he'd been. It was like therapy, and I couldn't wait for the next meeting.

Saying my goodbyes to my new friends, I offered to walk Hazel and Iris to their dorm. They giggled, then took me up on my offer. Each girl flanked me, slid an arm through each of mine and we reviewed our favorite moments of the night as we walked.

Once they were back safe and I was in my room, I stripped off the outfit and hung it lovingly in my closet like the prized possession it had become. And, for an hour after, I laid in my bed, finding a new comfort in the dark silence and thought of the things I'd like to add to Ajax's story and wardrobe. I'd completely forgotten my initial mission to use the group to learn more about vampires. Instead, it had become a sweet escape from my constant desire to push myself and cure a condition that I wasn't even sure existed anymore.

Rolling over, I settled into a comfortable position and waited for sleep to take me. The first semester had taught me that the brain was complex. I had to face the fact that I'd had a traumatic childhood. My memories of Sheena could be the poor recollection of a terrified child, wishing for a way out, mixed with the things I'd read in occult books. My utter belief in vampires came from a book that was sandwiched between aliens and palm reading. I had to admit that my ideas were as fanciful and fantastic as the ones we'd played out tonight. If the experience had taught me one thing, it was this, vampires were likely just as made up as fairies, dragons, the lady of the lake and unicorns.

The rest of winter break flew by. I spent the days lifting, shopping with Hazel for our costumes and coming up more ideas for stories. Sometimes the group would meet up for breakfast or a daytime hangout. At night, we played. Since no one had classes or went home, we could play as much as we wanted. Not all of the group came every night. Tony, Marie and Julian all had jobs so they sometimes couldn't play. Amanda and Heather went away one week for a romantic getaway. But we always had enough to play, then updated anyone who missed.

As the end of winter break came, we all lamented about the end of our fun. We'd still meet Monday, Wednesday and Friday but we knew that homework and the return of the whole campus would dampen the fun. During the holidays, we'd essentially had full run of the grounds. But, the return of our fellow students would mean taming down our play.

The afternoon before classes started, we picked up Isaac at the station. I was ashamed with how disappointed I felt to see my friend. Hazel ran to his arms as I hung back, letting them have their reunion. When he came to me, the hug was genuine. It wasn't that I wished he wasn't back, it was more that it signaled the end of our fun. I also knew that I had to tell him everything but wasn't sure how to or when. I needed to talk to Hazel first, but we couldn't sneak around behind his back to play, it wasn't right to keep it all from him.

We got dinner and Isaac told us all about his time away. He'd gotten a new guitar for Christmas that he couldn't wait to break in and had written a song for Hazel. The stories of his family sounded like the perfect mix of loving and funny. I was quickly remembering why I liked him so much and saw from the way the two looked at each other that they were way past "like."

Once back in the dorm, I left to give them a few hours alone and found myself in the library. I think it was a force of habit. The facility was open for anyone wanting an early start to the semester, but the librarian behind the counter looked very unhappy to be back to work. I wandered the stacks, trying to find something that would hold my interest until it closed.

"Ajax." I instinctually turned, not really processing that I'd responded to a name that wasn't truly mine. Julian sat in an arm chair in the back corner of the room, glasses on, legs crossed and a book in his lap. I smiled and crossed to sit in the chair next to his. "What are you doing here?"

"Roommate has his girlfriend over," I explained. "You?"

"Funny enough," he winked. "Same thing. Must be something in the air."

He pulled the glasses up to rest on the top of his head. Without the contacts from the game, I saw that his eyes were the same brown as his hair. In the game, he wore a wig that was the same shade as his natural hair but was braided down to his low back. I always wondered what it would be like to have hair that long but knew I'd never have the patience for it. I was actively growing mine out but never wanted it longer than my shoulders. Maybe I'd try on his wig some time, just to see what I would look like.

"What's up, man?" He asked. "What thought are you lost in?"

"Oh," I tried to laugh it off. "I just space out sometimes. What are you reading?"

He flipped the book to show me. "Dante's Inferno. Getting ahead of this semester's reading."

"I haven't really been able to talk to you outside of game. What's your major?"

He looked embarrassed. "Lit. You?"

"Pre-med," I answered.

He sucked air through his teeth. "Yikes. I knew it was going to be something smart like that."

I laughed. "I don't know about smart. I've basically volunteered for like 15 years of school. What do you want to do with a lit degree? Are you a writer?"

"I've written some things, but I don't know. I just love books and stories and thought it would be fun to study. Maybe I'll teach or maybe I'll get this degree and do nothing with it."

"Are you first year?"

"Second," he winked again. "So, there's still time to change course."

He was so easy to talk to. He told me about starting the game the previous year, how the game master was even better than Drew but had graduated. He asked me about medicine and why I chose it, with me giving the standard line of wanting to help people. We both came from small towns full of people with small minds and had dreamed of bigger things. Only the librarian starting to turn off lights let us know we'd have to end our conversation.

"Which dorm are you in?" I asked. "Do you need more time before you can go back?"

"I'm off campus, in an apartment. One of the perks of not being a freshman," he chuckled. "But it means needing a car so it's not for everyone." He checked his watch. "Are you heading back? I can walk with you."

"Yeah," I said. "Whether they're done or not, I need to get some sleep to be ready for tomorrow's chaos."

We exited the library, and the librarian clicked the lock the second we were out. Several people walked around the campus, reuniting with friends and preparing for classes to start in less than 12 hours. As much as I missed the still of the break, it was nice to see my university come back to life. Julian continued to ask me about myself, and I continued to dodge the questions by asking some of my own. When we reached my building, he paused and faced me. I noticed then that he wasn't much shorter than me. He extended his hand, and I took it to shake but he held on. "Well, Ajax, this was nice. I'm glad I got to know you better."

"Me too," I responded and really meant it. "Maybe we can meet up outside of the game again?"

"I'd like that." His grin was hiding something, but I wasn't sure what. Then he turned and strode away, leaving me to ponder what I was feeling.

Thankfully, Isaac and Hazel were asleep, so they'd had the time they needed, and I wasn't interrupting. Heading to the bathroom to brush my teeth, I replayed the night in my head. To my surprise, I'd felt a kind of loss watching Julian walk away. Was I attracted to him? I'd known gay men existed but had never met one or even suspected I was. Or was he just interesting and I genuinely wanted to hang out with him again? Staring into my reflection, I tried to understand the way he'd made me feel but couldn't. I told myself that I didn't need to figure it out that night and was probably just tired and feeling lonely.

I'd even convinced myself that was all it was, until the vivid dream of Julian and I doing more than talking told me there was more to this than just good conversation.

14

Spring semester was in full swing. We hit the ground running, quickly falling back into our routine of breakfast together, breaking for classes and seeing each other at night. The second night of the semester was an evening when the game was in play. Hazel went but I didn't. I told myself it was because I didn't feel right playing without telling Isaac. Deep down, I think I was hesitant to see Julian again, confused about my feelings towards him. When Hazel asked me what to tell the group, I told her I needed a couple days to get the hang of my new classes before adding play back in. She was obviously disappointed but agreed to go without me.

That next morning, at breakfast, I waited for Isaac to go for his usual second plate and then asked her, "When are we going to tell him about the group? It feels wrong to not tell him."

She looked surprised. "Alex, I already told him."

Shocked, I looked over to my roommate who was scooping scrambled eggs onto a waffle. "Really?" I asked her.

"Yeah," she arched an eyebrow. "It's not his kind of thing but he's cool with us playing. I tell him everything.

Guilt overwhelmed me, but I chose to face it head on when my friend returned. "So, you know that Hazel and I are playing Raven Realm?"

He smiled and bobbed his head. "Of course."

"And you don't mind?" I asked, still shocked at how cool he was about his girlfriend and I doing something without him.

"Nah, man," he slapped my shoulder. "It makes you guys happy so why wouldn't I be happy for you? And while you two play, I can practice some more so it's win-win."

"I don't know," I admitted. "I felt like we were leaving you out or something."

His laugh was genuine. "That's nice, Alex. But I promise I don't feel left out. It's not my kind of thing but no judgement. I'd love to see your outfits though. Hazel has told me all about it and it sounds awesome."

I looked to her and she was beaming at him. "How about we show you tomorrow night?"

He took her hand. "I would love that."

Clearly, she'd meant it when she said she told him everything. While he finished his meal and I sipped at my coffee, I thought about the healthiness of it all. I'd only really had my parents as examples of what a couple was like. Was this what relationships were supposed to be? Honesty and acceptance and allowing each other to just be themselves? And if it was, then did I want that with someone?

My watch beep broke my thoughts before I could answer my own question. I jumped up. "Oh shit. I gotta get to Anatomy. Can you take this cup up for me?"

"You got it," Isaac answered to my back as I grabbed my bag and speed-walked to the science hall. Once in class, I might as well have skipped the lecture, I was so lost in my own head. Now, that the excuse of Isaac not knowing our game was gone, I had to face that I was nervous to see Julian again. But, why? I mean, if what I felt was attraction, what did that mean? And I didn't even know that was what it was. Maybe, I really just thought he was cool and wanted to hang out more. The only way to know for sure, was to see him and I could do that by returning to the game the next night.

And, then what? I mean, we weren't ourselves once the game was in play. Before and after, we were surrounded by people so it wasn't like I could really get to know him. It had taken weeks and a chance encounter at the library to start a simple conversation. There was only one way to figure out what I was feeling and that was to hang out alone again.

So, that was the plan. Go to the game the next night, ask him to hang out and make a plan. Simple and easy. The worst thing that happened was he said no.

And truthfully, I didn't know if I wanted him to say no or yes.

I saac left the room when I got ready the next night. He seemed to be just as excited to see us as he said. He wanted to wait until I was in full garb. My hair was past my ears, and I had to admit it did add to the look. But it was the heavy cloak Tony had given me that really made me look like the medieval warrior. I'd tried to give him money, but he'd sworn he'd been given the cloak by a graduating senior, and it had just hung in his closet because it was too big. "I'm happy to have the space in my closet back and for it to go to someone who can use it," he'd said when he bought it to me the previous day.

A rap at the door hit my ears as it was opening. Isaac stepped in and clapped his hands at the sight. "Dude," he shouted. "You look incredible. Worth all the early workouts." I bought my arms out of the heavy fabric and twirled to show him the whole thing. When my spin ended and my eyes hit his, I knew he'd seen the scars. It was only a second, just a flash of pain, but it was there, and I'd seen it.

He gathered himself. "Just amazing, man. You look like you could kick some ass."

I made the choice to pretend he hadn't seen what he had, that they didn't bother me, and I gave him a dramatic sweeping bow. "I thank you."

Before the air could get anymore awkward, I was saved by Hazel's entrance. She wore the same outfit I'd seen her in the first night and Isaac's hand flew to his heart. "Wow," he said. "Just wow."

She giggled, came to the center of the room and gave him the same spin that I'd just performed. Then, she curtsied. "Sire." When she came back up, Isaac crossed to her, wrapped his arm around her waist and kissed her. I expected her to say something about ruining her makeup, but she clearly didn't care. They locked eyes, then you could see an idea cross his eyes. "Picture?"

"Huh," I asked.

He rummaged through his bag and pulled out a disposable camera. "Can I take your picture?" Hazel and I exchanged a look, shrugged and came together. Isaac led us out into the night and pointed to a massive oak tree in the center of the quad. It was bathed in a streetlight and a perfect place for us to pose, a warrior and witch under an ancient tree. He snapped a few pictures and sent us on our way to have fun.

It wasn't until we hit the door of the rec building that my nerves started to rumble through my body. "Cold?" Hazel asked me. I lied and told her yes as we shuffled into the foyer and down the hall. I heard the familiar music and the murmur of several voices having several conversations. Stepping into the room, I saw Julian immediately. He was talking to Iris about something, and she was enamored with whatever he was saying. He was in his full game, Aramus, attire. The brown wig was a massive braid down his ruby red tunic, which made his skin all the more pale. Mid-sentence, his sparkling emerald eyes side-gazed to me. He didn't miss a beat in his story, while he shifted his view to me, smirked and then returned to the tiny fairy. Heat roiled through my abdomen, spreading down my limbs and out. Whatever I'd felt that night outside my dorm was intensified by the makeup, contacts, costume and long hair. I told myself that that's all it was, and it didn't change my plan to spend time out of game getting to know him.

When the whole group had arrived, they updated myself and the two others who'd skipped the previous game on what we'd missed. Drew had a twist coming and asked us all to please be ready for what was to come, cautioning us to stay in game even if we didn't like it and wait until after game to talk to him. A knot twisted in my stomach simultaneously with a flutter in my chest for what the surprise may be. He sent us all into the night with an ominous warning to "watch out for each other and also trust no one."

My instinct was to separate from the group and find a place to watch what was happening before I decided what to do next. I was deep in the woods that surrounded the campus when I heard "in game" called out into the air. The dark cloak helped me blend into the shadows and dropping to the ground made me harder to find. However, my vantage point was up a hill, so I could watch everyone move around without giving away my location.

Hazel and Iris, forever together in the game, huddled together. They danced down a sidewalk like nothing bad could ever get them and their magic would be enough. Several others had set up a sort of camp, thinking that numbers would keep them safe. I saw Drew and Chris off in a corner whispering and I knew Chris must be part of the twist we'd either love or hate. I was much too far to hear any of the players, but I'd chose sight over words any day.

"Good spot," the whisper was so low that it took a moment to recognize it was real. Turning slowly, as to not disturb the dead leaves under my knees, I saw only green eyes in the darkness. "Ajax, I mean you no harm."

Nodding once, I watched Julian/Aramus seem to silently slide from the shadows to my side. "I see our game master has chosen his enemy for the evening."

I swallowed hard, trying to find the air to talk. "You think he will be our enemy? But he's one of us."

Aramus arched an eyebrow, smirking in a way that hid secrets. "Is he, though?"

I turned to watch Drew and Chris but didn't care about what they were up to. I was just trying to give myself some time to think. With the man right next to me, I couldn't pretend that the effect he had on me wasn't real. It was like being starved and knowing a slice of chocolate cake sat next to you. I wanted to reach out and grab him, but wasn't sure for what purpose.

"They plan to grab one of the girls," he whispered into my ear. "He's going to grab her and offer her to the Dark for a price. He owes a great deal of coin to a bad man and is desperate. He's not a bad vampire." I tried to focus on his words but my heart pounding in my ears. "But desperation is worse than having ill intent. Don't you think?"

He was so close, and it was taking away my logical thought second by second. My head was swimming. The heat filling my body made me want to rip off my cloak. But something occurred to me. "How could you know that? You can't hear them from here." Pulling together my waning strength, I turned to face him again. He smiled. "How do I know you aren't working with them? It's clear to me you're hiding something."

Laughter rolled out of his throat without concern for being heard. His chest swelled underneath with the power of his laugh, making the crimson tunic stretch. I was mesmerized by his colors: the red fabric, the green of his eyes, his coffee braid and his white skin. It was perfect skin, ivory and flawless. I ran my gaze over his hands, neck, face to be sure I was seeing what I was seeing. Without thought, I scrambled away from him, really seeing him for the first time.

He froze, mid-laugh, his eyes growing wide. He knew that I knew.

"The hair, the eyes. It can't," my throat was seizing with fear, my mouth was dry. "It's not possible."

"Alex," he cautioned. "Don't do this."

"You're a vampire."

16

Julian moved faster than I could see, just on the ground one second then upright and standing over me the next. He grabbed my arm and pulled me to my feet like I weighed nothing. His hand felt like ice over my mouth. "Do not speak another word," he snapped. "Not here." He looked down to the quad and we watched Chris burst from a hedge to grab Lucy as she passed. She shrieked and the larger group that had made camp, ran to fight for her.

"I'm going to move my hand and you're going to listen. Got it?" I nodded and he dropped his hand. "Do not speak to anyone about this. Finish the game, then meet me in the parking lot. Got it?" I nodded again, opening my mouth to ask a question. But he was gone before the first word left my lips.

Shaking overtook me. Could that have really happened? I had no doubt about my sanity and had never had delusions before, so why would I now? But it was absurd, right? An actual vampire playing a vampire game surrounded by humans pretending to be vampires? I mean, it was too ridiculous.

I worked my way down to the group, only halfway listening to what was being said. It was clear that Chris' attempt to betray us and take a girl to the Dark Provence had been thwarted. He was tied to a tree while the others celebrated their victory. Someone slapped my back and asked me where I had been when they really needed me. I shrugged, unable to come up with even a simple sentence. "You okay?" Hazel asked and I nodded weakly.

Drew called end of game and someone set Chris free. They were all deciding what to do with his character next game when I told Hazel I wasn't feeling well and walked away from the crowd, ignoring the questions about where I was going. My feet worked independently of my brain, heading for the parking lot even as my brain was telling me that going to meet up with a vampire was the dumbest thing I could ever do.

When I turned the corner, I saw him standing next to his car and wondered why I ever thought he was human. Everything about him was inhuman if you really looked. His movement were too smooth, his face too perfect, his eyes too wise for his apparent age. Even his smile was just a little too wonderful. "I can't believe you came," he said, opening his passenger door for me to climb in.

What am I doing, I thought. But I didn't say a word when he climbed in, started the engine and backed out of the lot. It occurred to me that no one knew where I was going or who I was with. Yet, I still said nothing during the drive. Quickly, I tried to remember everything I'd ever read about vampires. If any of it was true, I was already dead. He would be stronger, faster and smarter than me. I recalled the information on possible powers and wondered if I wasn't speaking because he was using magic on me.

"You're not talking," he said. "Because you're in shock and still don't believe this is real."

He was staring forward, eyes on the road, with no hint of amusement in his gaze. "Did you just read my mind?"

"I did," he smirked. "Still don't believe what you know is true?"

"How can this be?" I asked.

"That's a complicated question which I'll try to answer, but first tell me this." He pulled into a driveway of a small house and killed the engine. "And, it's a waste of time to lie." He waited for me to nod before continuing. "How do you know about vampires? And how did you know about me?"

"My sister is a vampire."

I don't think he was expecting that answer and shock filled his eyes. "Interesting. Come inside. We need to talk."

He was out the door, up the front steps and inside the house before I found the strength to unbuckle my seatbelt. Was I going to do this? Was I going to voluntarily walk into the house of a thing that could kill me? My feet answered for me, following the same path Julian had just taken and through the open door. Closing it behind me, I saw a modest living room. A grey couch sat against a wall with books piled next to it. Simple paintings hung here and there, a TV sat covered in dust and he was squat down in front of a fire place, filling it with crumpled newspaper. A tuxedo cat came out from an adjacent room and rubbed against Julian while he struck the match and touched it to the paper. Once logs were placed on top, he picked up the cat, stood, turned to me and asked me to sit.

When we were both on the couch, he laid the cat in his lap to doze off. It was he that broke the silence. "I don't know if it's cold in here, so if the fire isn't enough, you have to tell me."

"Okay," I was still having trouble accepting the reality I was in.

"So," he slowly stroked the cat, and its purr had a sort of calming effect on me. "Tell me about your sister."

Swallowing, I opened my mouth and the whole story just poured out of me. I told him about her disappearance, what my parents had told everyone, the police not caring and her arriving at my window. When it was done, I noticed my fear had abated. I wasn't exactly comfortable next to him, but at least my heart rate was somewhere within normal limits. "How did you know she was a vampire?" he asked.

"I didn't" I admitted. "At least not at the time. No one believed me except my friend Norman." A pang hit my gut with the mention of his name. I hadn't called him once since I left, and I knew it was a terrible repayment for all his years of friendship, but it seemed so much less important now that I was facing a vampire. "It wasn't until last year, when I found this vampire book, that I knew what had happened to her, why she acted like that."

"And," he pushed. "Where is she now?"

"I don't know," I said. "I haven't seen her since that night."

He stopped petting the cat, but it didn't care, it was asleep. "And, how did you know I was one?"

Another hard swallow. There was no point in lying, he'd made that clear. "I didn't, not at first. You hide it well but," I stopped.

"But, what?" He turned and I felt his eyes on me like a blade against my skin.

"Tonight, in the light." I faced him, trying to not let him see how unnerved I truly was. "You're too perfect. Your skin is flawless; the eyes are better than any contact and there is no circle around them from a lens."

"Hm," he hummed, and I didn't know if it was amusement or frustration.

"So," I gathered my courage to ask what I wanted to know. "The way I saw you in the library? That's the fake look, right? And this is the real you?"

"It is," he admitted. I waited for more, but he wasn't going to just give it up. He was waiting for me to ask.

"Your hair? It's really that long?"

Julian smiled in a way that warmed me, genuine joy. He reached behind his back, pulling the braid to the front, releasing the hair from the tie and undoing the plait. The cat was angered by his movements, jumping down to go sleep elsewhere. When the hair was freed, it shined in a way that no shampoo could give you. Instinctually, I reached out, then froze. "Go ahead," he offered.

It was like satin through my fingers, all that hair, and I wondered yet again how I ever thought he was human. Dropping my hand, I pulled it into me.

"Why hide it?" It sounded stupid out loud, but I was curious.

"Because we're meant to blend," he answered, making me feel foolish for asking. "Within the game, I get to drop the masking and be myself. Everyone thinks I'm in costume, as they are." He leaned into me. "Except you," he smiled. "You saw."

My muscles shook with the need to pull back from him, but I held my spot. "It's too good," I answered.

He slowly shook his head. "No," he sighed. "No. You see me better than all the other humans. I've been doing this a long time, yet I couldn't fool you. I knew as soon as I saw you that there is something different about you. What is it?"

I didn't like this line of questioning. Was he angry that I'd figured it out? Was I in danger? Would he let me leave this house?

"You're not in danger, Alex." He leaned back so I could catch my breath. "Just be honest. How did you see me so well?"

"I don't know," I admitted and knew he could read in my thoughts that I really didn't know. Did other humans not see how obvious it was? "Maybe it's because I know what to look for."

"Maybe," he relented.

"Can I ask you something?" I knew I was pushing it, but this was a rare opportunity and the scientist in me was hungry for knowledge.

"Sure," he waved his hand.

"Why be in the group?"

He laughed. "You mean why am I pretending to be a human pretending to be a vampire?"

"Yeah," I agreed. "What is the point?"

"Well," he clapped his hands onto his thighs. "I moved here and enrolled because I was bored. I wanted to learn something new in a new town, you know?" He looked at me and I nodded. "When I asked for permission to come to this town, the Lady asked me to join the group and see what they knew, if it was something to worry about."

"Lady?" I asked.

"Um," he searched my face, trying to decide if he should say more. "The one of us that's in charge of this area. For your sake, that's all you need to know. Got it?" I nodded. "So, I joined and quickly realized it was really nothing to worry about. I let her know but she asked me to stay in, just in case. It seemed like a small price to pay for a new town and new start, so I stayed in." He stopped but then decided to say more. "Honestly, they're not bad kids and I have fun playing."

I thought about what he'd said, about wanting a new start and being bored. "How old are you?" I didn't think he'd answer but, again, my curiosity won over my good sense.

He stared at me for a moment, unblinking, contemplating. "Just over 100." He said it like he worried I would run screaming from the room. When I didn't, he continued. "How old are you?"

"Almost 19" I answered in the same tone, and we sat in silence, him contemplating my youth and I contemplating an existence a century long with infinite more to go.

It was he that spoke next. "Are you scared?"

I had to think about it, search my system to know for sure. I was surprised by the truth. "No," I shook my head. "Should I be?"

"Depends." I didn't like that word but waited to see what followed. "Can I trust you?"

"You can," and I knew he could read it in my mind, so I just said it aloud. "I don't know your story and I don't know how Sheena was turned but I know I wouldn't do anything to hurt you guys unless you give me a reason to."

He seemed amused. "And, if I did? What could you do about it?"

"Good point," I admitted it. "Can I trust you? To not hurt me?"

"You can," he smirked. "Unless you make me."

I extended my hand, and he grasped it to shake. "Deal."

I was trying to lighten the situation, but he gripped me tight, pulling me into him to lock eyes with me. "Alex," his voice had taken on a new quality, I could feel it in my chest. "This is serious. The others can't know that you know the truth. They won't like a human in our town being able to pick out who is a vampire and who is not."

"Others," I asked. "There are more?"

"There are many," he let go of my hand. "And most of them are not as nice as me."

17

Julian let me take his car to return to campus, with the plan for me to join him at his house the next night for more conversation. Slipping into my room, I heard the soft sounds of Isaac sleeping in the darkness. Stripping down, I slid under my blankets to replay the night in my mind.

A vampire, on campus, in our games, amongst humans with no one the wiser. Well, no one but me. And why did that upset Julian so much? That I figured it out? Could he have been telling the truth when he said I shouldn't have been able to?

My cells were vibrating. I wanted it to be the next night so I could return to him. I had so many questions, but he made it clear he needed to rest during the day and would tell me more after sunset. So, that part of the lore was true. Vampires couldn't be out in the day. Only I wanted more details, like would they burn in the sun? Did they sleep in coffins or boxes of dirt? I made the mental note to start writing down all my questions so I wouldn't miss anything.

Finally, exhaustion overtook me, and a dreamless sleep was my reward for making it through the night. When I opened my eyes, I was confused at first. It was much brighter than it should have been. When I looked at the clock, I realized why. I'd forgotten an alarm and slept until noon. My first two classes of the day were over. I leapt from bed, pulling on the first shirt and jeans I could find, running out the door with my shoe laces flopping around each frantic step.

I made it to the lunch hall just in time to see Hazel and Isaac sit in our usual spot. Crossing to them and skidding to a halt, they both look startled. "I never thought I'd see the day where Alex missed classes. Good morning," Hazel joked.

I dropped into an open seat and Isaac slid his coffee to me. "Late night?" he asked.

"Yeah," I sighed, not sure what I was going to tell them if they asked any more.

"Feel any better?" Hazel asked. I'd forgotten about telling her I didn't feel well.

"Oh, yeah," I lied. "I think I slept it off. I feel fine. Listen" I prepared for more lying. "I'm going to study with someone tonight so you two can have the room to yourself. I won't be back until really late."

They exchanged glances and I could see they were excited for a night alone. "That's cool," Isaac laid his hand on Hazel's then looked at me. "But you know we love hanging out with you. Don't leave just for us."

"I'm not," I assured them and knew nothing could stop me from my plans that night.

"Who are you studying with?" Isaac asked.

I cleared my throat, not sure what to say. But, it's not like I was told I couldn't say *who* just not *what*, right? "Julian."

"From the group?" Hazel perked up. I nodded. "Oh Alex. Iris has such a crush on him. Can you get intel for her? Like does he have a girlfriend? How old he is? All that? He doesn't talk much when we're all together. Real quiet, you know?"

I gulped at the room temp coffee to buy me some time and hide my amusement. I figured Iris wouldn't mind an older man, but this was probably too much of an age gap. Hazel's eyes were pleading so I needed to say something. "Sure," I shrugged, and she squealed. I figured I could come up with something later to deter Iris, like saying he was gay or had an STD. I'd ask him what gossip he'd prefer.

"Weird," Hazel said. "I didn't peg Julian for a science major. Seemed more like a poetry guy."

I nodded again, not sure what do say or how deep I wanted to dig this hole of lies. "He is actually," I figured the more accuracy the better. "He's a lit major. He's going to help me with my American Lit class so I can get this English credit out of the way and focus on my bio stuff."

She smiled. "I knew it." She leaned into Isaac. "I'm really good at reading people. I almost think I'm psychic sometimes. I'm so intuitive."

I coughed into the last of the coffee and pretended it was a tickle in my throat and not me snickering at how off Hazel was about Julian. My watch alarm saved me from any more questions. I thanked my roommate for sacrificing his coffee to me and told them I'd see them in the morning. Then rushed off for my afternoon classes.

Every minute of class moved at an agonizingly slow pace. The droning of each lecture was more hypnotic sound than an actual lesson. I spent most of my time scribbling questions for Julian into my notebook, which probably looked like me taking notes. I didn't know if he'd answer any of these, but I knew I had to try and take advantage of this. The fire I felt within me to find the cure for vampirism was hotter than ever. What were the odds that I'd come across someone who could tell me more than any book? College would prepare me for the practice of medicine and teach me about the human body. But only an actual vampire could help me understand their species, and the universe had put one in my path.

I was so caught up in the idea that I had a way to enter the world of the vampires that I didn't stop to ask myself if I should.

I was knocking on Julian's door ten minutes after sundown. I didn't know how much time a vampire needed post-daylight. Like, did they snap awake when the sun dropped out of the sky or need time to come to like humans? I added that to my list of questions and prepared to wait on the porch for however long he needed.

The door opened and no one was there. From within, I heard him say "You can come in, Alex."

Stepping in, I saw that no one was there yet the door closed. From a back room, Julian emerged with a full glass in each hand. Both contained a dark liquid, and I was afraid to ask. "One is wine for you and the other is blood for me. Living room?"

"Oh, um, sure." I removed my coat to hang on the coat rack and looked at my shoes, deciding to kick them off out of a need to have good manners and seeing Julian was barefoot. I had walked across his carpet with shoes on the previous night, but I could blame shock for that. There was no excuse now.

"Thank you," Julian smiled. "That's nice of you. Come, sit." He sat in the same place he'd sat the night before and I liked the familiarity of it. It made me feel safer to have a routine with him. "Do you need the fire?" He asked.

"Actually," I admitted. "No, it's really warm in here."

"Good," he sat the glass for me on the coffee table and started to sip at his. "If it gets uncomfortable for you, you will tell me? I've never had a human in here."

I sat, taking the wine and sipping at it. I didn't want him to know that I'd never had wine and hoped I didn't react in a way to show him. To my surprise, it was smooth on my throat and the flavor exploded in my mouth in a way I enjoyed. "Mmm," I said aloud and wished I hadn't. It felt immature but it seemed to please him.

"That's a red blend from California. It was a favorite of someone I used to know, so I have many bottles." He sipped at his while I took another drink of mine.

"Um," I wanted to ask but felt it to be rude.

"Go ahead," he urged.

"I have to say this because I promised. Iris likes you and I've been tasked with finding out if you like her."

He smiled. "I know. I can smell her desire, but she is much too young, and I won't be with any more humans, too messy. They're drawn to us without knowing why. But, it's up to us to not let them fall into our beds, not let them crave something that could destroy them. You understand?" He looked at me and I realized he wasn't just talking about Iris. He wanted me to understand that he and I would remain platonic. I blushed, unsure if I was embarrassed, disappointed or relieved.

"I'll tell her you're gay," I blurted out. He smiled and I wasn't sure if he was pleased or amused. I wanted to change the subject fast. I gestured to his glass. "That's blood?"

"It is," he took a last gulp and sat the glass down. I watched the remnants of the blood slide back from the rim to the bottom.

"So, that's real."

"That's not what you want to ask," he prodded. I realized how useless it was to try and hide my thoughts from someone who could read them.

"How do you get it?" I asked.

He licked his lips. "We each play a part in our community. Some of us can get blood and provide it to others."

I finished off my wine, letting the heat of it embolden me. "What do you do for the community?"

His smile told me he was pleased with my question and proud of what he was about to say. "Many of us need to get degrees to find gainful employment in this new world. Before, we could get away with other ways of making money but it's getting harder, especially for the new ones." He reached to the side of the couch, picking up a wine bottle from the floor, uncorking it and pouring more into my glass. The aroma was sweet, like berries. I picked up my glass and sipped at it. "I have studied many subjects, earned many degrees. So, I help the others enroll and pass, teach them new technologies and aid them in acclimating to higher education amongst humans."

The wine was starting make me feel relaxed. "Like a vampire guidance counselor."

His laughter was so rich, it rolled down my body in a similar heat to what the wine did. "I love that, Alex. A vampire guidance counselor. Yes."

"I have so many questions," I pulled my notebook from my backpack and Julian clapped a hand on my back.

"A whole notebook, then?" He asked. "How about this," he offered. "I answer a question, then you answer question? Only honesty between us. What is said in this room, stays in this room."

Just the thought of being vulnerable, being asked personal questions, made me squirm. Normally, I would have stood, told this person good night and walked back to the dorm. But, the wine and the promise of learning something that no human knew was too intoxicating. It felt like this wasn't real or didn't have real consequences, like I had nothing to lose. I gave in. "Deal."

"What does it feel like to be sick?" It was such a simple and complex question. How would I explain it?

"Depends on what kind of sick. There's so many. But I guess it feels like your body isn't working like it should. Your limbs can feel heavy or slow; your mind can slow down, too. Things inside you ache. Does that answer it for you?"

"Good enough," he relented.

"Do vampires have magical powers?" I wasn't sure how else to word it.

"Not really magic but yes, we each get one or two abilities. You know I can hear thoughts, and I can move objects with my mind, like the door tonight. Other vampires get other abilities. Many of us can mask, I mean change our appearance." I wanted to ask what kinds of abilities but needed to save it for another question.

"Who gave you the scars?" He asked with no ceremony.

"My father," I answered without hesitation and gave him no more. He'd have to use more questions if he wanted details.

"How are you made a vampire?" I wanted information and if I was going to give up my dearest held secrets to Julian, he was going to pay me back.

"Once you have little to no blood left, a moment before death, you drink your maker's blood and that makes you a vampire. Did you ever pay your father back for those scars?"

"No," I admitted and was relieved that it didn't fill me with shame anymore. Or, maybe, it was just Julian's presence or the red blend that took that shame away. "What is it like to be turned?"

"Painful, scary and wonderous all at once. Like being born but you see all the hardest parts of your life. Did you get so strong because of what your dad did to you?"

"Yes," and it was the truth. "Do you have a choice to turn or not?"

He arched his eyebrow. He was amused that I picked up this part in his description of the turning. "Yes," he smiled. "You can choose to die or turn. You have the time." Then he answered a question I didn't ask. "So, your sister chose to turn."

I swallowed a painful amount of air and used the wine to coat my throbbing throat. I needed a moment to let that revelation sink in. She'd chosen to turn, just like she'd chosen to leave me alone with our parents. "Why did you choose?"

I may have gone too far but I didn't care. He'd opened a wound with talking about Sheena and I was going to make him just as raw. He licked his lips and looked away. "For a woman."

I hadn't thought about what I may have revealed when I'd asked, only thought about paying him back. Now, seeing the pain in his eyes, I wished I could erase the previous minute. "I'm sorry," I whispered.

He turned to me and for the first time that night, his gaze matched the years he'd walked the Earth. "Don't be. I started this game, and I said honesty only."

"Where is she?" I asked.

"She is dead," he cocked his head to the side and a sad smile crossed his face. Then, he righted himself and joviality returned. "That was two, so I get two. What does the wine taste like and what does drunkenness feel like?"

I was taken aback. We were headed down a path of hard, serious questions so these silly queries took me aback. The earnestness in his eyes told me not to joke. "Um, well. The wine is like this sweetness with a hint of bitter. It's warm going down. Drunkenness is like that warmth taking over your whole body which then turns into a liquid peace. You stop worrying about anything and just exist in the moment. You've never had wine or felt drunk?"

"I have but memories fade. It sounds lovely," he sighed.

"It is," I admitted. "It's nice to not worry for a few hours. I don't care about my grades or my mission. I just relax."

"Your mission?" He alerted at my phrasing. "What is your mission?"

I emptied the wine glass and set it down with authority, willing myself to just say it. "I'm going to med school, becoming a hematologist, studying the vampire blood and developing a cure for vampirism. Then, I'm finding my sister and curing her."

My honesty was met with silence. I stood, grabbed the wine bottle, uncorked it and filled my glass again, sitting back down to let Julian process what I'd said. Minutes ticked by and I waited for him to tell me what he thought. I prepared myself for argument and warning. I expected him to tell me to stay out of vampire business or that it was impossible.

He broke the silence. "I want to help you."

"What do you mean?" I needed clarity on what helping me meant to him.

He stood and paced around the room like he was making the plan out loud. I listened, letting him verbalized his thoughts in real time. "I have a bio degree already. So, I'll keep studying literature while you finish pre-med, then get into med school. I go to the same med school, we learn together. You use my blood to test." He looked at me. "We could do this, figure out how to turn back vampirism."

"Why?" It was the only work I could think of.

"Because, Alex. I don't want to be a vampire anymore."

19

And, with that, I had a comrade in my mission to cure vampires who didn't want to be vampires anymore. We spent the rest of the night planning out our moves. Julian could get into any med school he wanted. He knew a vampire that could convince any dean into letting him in and convince every professor that he'd be in every class. So, once I was accepted, he'd come with me. We'd get a house together, to protect his identity. Any day classes, I could share my notes with him, and we'd get night rotations for his clinical hours.

It was nearing sunrise, when he'd realized how much time had gone by. "Please stay," he'd asked. "You haven't slept, and you finished that wine. I want you to be safe. Sleep in my spare room, when you wake, you can have the car again. I'll meet you at the group tonight."

I want more time to talk but knew I had to relent to the dawn and see him again that night. "Do you sleep in a coffin?" I had to know, and we were well past holding back.

He smiled. "Do you want to see?"

I did and grabbed my bookbag to follow him back. We headed down his hallway, and I realized I hadn't seen any of his house but his living room. Off to the right was a simple kitchen. No appliances sat on the counters since he didn't need anything but blood. It was odd to see no toaster, coffee maker, nothing. But it was useless to buy appliances when no one visited. Only the cat's food and water bowl reminded me that something mortal did share this space.

Next was a door to the left, which he opened to show a nicely made bed. "You can sleep here. It was furnished when I rented it, so I wash the bedding monthly, just in case." He took my bag and tossed it onto the bed. Then motioned for the door next to this one. "Bathroom." I nodded. He headed for the door at the end of the hallway, pausing with hand on doorknob. "Ready?" he asked, and I nodded again.

When the door swung open, I was shocked to see an ordinary bed. He laughed at my surprise. "Sorry, Alex. No coffin, just a bed and a thick blanket nailed over the window."

"Oh," I didn't leave the disappointment out of my voice.

"If it makes you feel better," he leaned in conspiratorially. "Some of the older ones do sleep in coffins and often they think less of those who don't." I laughed. "I would rather be in a nice bed, though. Wouldn't you?"

I thought about it and had to admit he was right. "Yeah, I guess I would."

He put his hand on my shoulder. "I'm trusting you with a great deal, Alex. Not just the information I've given you but letting you stay here while I sleep. I'm trusting you to not rip down that blanket or tell others about where I sleep. Many of us chose to protect our resting places for good reason."

The weight of his trust hit me. Without telling me, he was telling me he was vulnerable while he slept, and I knew the gravity of the situation. "You can trust me," I told him and meant it.

We went our separate ways. I'd learned that the cat was named Zeus when he'd joined his master on the bed just before I shut the door. I'd used the bathroom to wash up before I tried to sleep. I didn't know if I could rest after all that, but I knew I had to try. I was no good to myself or to our plan if I collapsed from exhaustion.

Lying in the empty room, I rolled everything around in my mind. For the first time, my goal of curing Sheena felt both real and attainable. With a vampire to help me, the possibilities were endless. His hope for a cure was so clear in his words and his eyes that it was contagious. His belief in me made me believe in myself. I was so certain that I'd find cure and see Julian step into the sun. I was so certain we'd then find my sister and give her the same.

Not for a second did it occur to me that neither would ever happen.

20

I'd dozed off around five am, so my alarm three hours later was like a drill to my brain. The remnants of the wine were sour in my stomach, my head felt ten pounds heavier, and my eyes burned with the need for sleep. The classes I'd missed the previous morning were not the same I had this morning so I could skip but I knew this was a slippery slope to keep missing classes. With my newfound hope for a cure, I knew I had to graduate with my bio degree to get into med school and the better the school record, the better my chances. So, I found the strength to grab my bag, get to Julian's car and return to campus.

Thankfully, this class day was light, and I was back in my dorm by lunch time to sleep off my late night. It was Isaac who woke me at the end of the day by flipping on the lights.

"Hey Alex, how was studying?"

"Good," I grumbled, trying to adjust to the sudden luminosity and sound. "How was your night with Hazel?"

He flopped onto his back on his bed. "Also good, man. I also didn't get much sleep, but it was so worth it. You?"

"Yeah," I admitted. "It was worth it. I feel like I know way more than I did before."

"That's great. Sounds like you and Julian meeting was meant to be."

I chuckled. He didn't know how right he was. What are the odds that a human who knows about vampires would meet one of the few who didn't mind talking to humans? And now I had a plan for reaching a goal what was almost impossible until a few days ago.

Isaac sat up on his bed, squaring his shoulders. "Um, I gotta tell you something and I'm not sure how."

I sat up, taken aback by the seriousness in his voice. "What is it?"

He rubbed the back of his neck. "Well, Hazel and I, we're getting kind of serious. And, last night, we we're talking. We're thinking about getting an off-campus apartment next year, her and I."

"Wow," I shook my head. "I mean, that's great you guys. I'm so happy for you."

"You can get a place with us, you know. We could get a two bed-room and you in one, us in the other. We really want you there, man, but we get it if you're not comfortable."

"Oh," I hadn't expected that. I figured they'd want the place to themselves. "That's so nice, but can I think about it? My scholarship covers dorms, but I don't think it covers rent off-campus."

"Yeah," he bobbed his head. "I get that and it's totally cool either way. Just let us know. We don't want anyone else. So, if you're in we'll get a two bedroom, if not only one. We just need to know by like June."

"Yeah, of course," I nodded, knowing damn well I couldn't afford off campus housing. My scholarship covered the meal plan, my dorms and my tuition. The money Mr. Crawford had given me was stretching but it wouldn't cover rent. It reminded me that I needed to call Norman. I grabbed my wall calendar and flipped to the end of May. By then, his first year would be done, he'd be home, and I could spend all summer catching up with him.

I obviously wouldn't talk about Julian, but I could tell him about my classes, Isaac, Hazel and our LARP group. He'd probably love that

I was role playing and I could already hear the jokes he'd make about me being a nerd.

I hustled to dinner to eat something before getting ready for the game play that night. I hadn't eaten since the previous night and was starving. I ate three plates full, uncommon for me, but I knew I needed calories to get through the night. I vowed to go straight to bed after the group, and save the late nights with Julian for non-school nights like Friday and Saturday.

And, that was exactly how it went for the rest of spring semester. I played Raven Realm Monday, Wednesday and Fridays. I went to Julian's on Friday and Saturday nights so we could talk, and Isaac and Hazel could be alone. Tuesdays and Thursdays I studied, did homework and got sleep.

By final exams, I felt like I nothing could stop me. I was so locked in that I wasn't surprised to see a 4.0 on my transcript when I picked it up. Hazel and Isaac weren't mad when I told them I couldn't move with them and had picked a one-bedroom apartment walkable from campus. Instead of risking a weird roommate for the following year, Julian had begged me to move into his spare room. He'd insisted on it, saying that having someone living around the house was good for him and Zeus. He even bought a window air conditioner for my room. I'd found out I could take the dorm stipend from my scholarship to put towards rent after I'd told Isaac and Hazel I couldn't live with them. I'd offered it to Julian, but he refused and told me to use it for "human stuff."

When the semester wrapped, I'd helped Hazel and Isaac move their things into their apartment. They'd offered to help me move, but I told them I didn't need it, not sure how to explain that Julian was protective of his home. I'd thought they'd be offended when they found out I was living with him and not them, but they didn't ask any questions. I think they'd secretly wanted to live alone.

I used the last week of May to transfer my small collection of possessions to Julian's spare room, get a phone line and cable, then settle into a summer routine. The LARP group was in hiatus until September, so it was more free time to focus on my goals. I was taking a few classes over the summer to graduate faster and started a new workout plan to take advantage of the free time when I didn't have class and Julian was sleeping.

The second week of June, I finally sat down to call the Crawfords. I'd been procrastinating, feeling so guilty for letting a whole year go by. I was thinking of what excuse I'd give those amazing people for not staying in touch. It was time to just call. I poured Zeus' dinner into his bowl, extracted the receiver from the wall phone and dialed the number by heart. It rang a few times as I sat at the kitchen table and rolled my finger around the cord. To my relief, it was Mr. Crawford who answered and not his wife. I knew her allegiance was to my mother, and she'd run across the street to tell her I'd called them and not my parents.

"Hello?" his gruff voice blasted a smile across my face. I'd thought about a thousand things to say to him but needed to ease into this reunion.

"Mr. Crawford, it's Alex. I'm hoping Norman is home for the summer and we can start catching up. I can't wait to hear about his first year."

Silence met my question. He was mad at me, I knew it. Norman had probably told him that I'd never called, and Mr. Crawford knew I'd taken his money and years if his kindness without gratitude.

I tried to fix it. "I know I should have called before, but I've been so busy. I know that's not an excuse and I feel awful, but I want to make up for lost time."

"Alex," he cleared his throat. "Norman isn't here."

"Oh," I sighed. "Did he stay on campus? I did too. Can I have his number or give you mine and you can pass it on to him?" I pulled open kitchen drawer to look for a pencil and paper, finding neither. I did find a pen and ran it across my palm to make sure it would work before Mr. Crawford spoke again.

"Alex," his voice broke. "Norman is dead."

21

My vision swam and I sat to the ground before my knees could give out. The phone cord was taut; the receiver was silent. Zeus ran up to me, thinking that my presence on the floor was an invitation. He climbed into my lap, curling up to purr and sleep off his feast. Julian walked in to see me on the floor and looked confused, probably trying to understand if all humans talked into the phone while on the ground.

"What?" I managed into the dead air.

"He's dead, Alex. Your parents said they told you. I should've known better, those selfish pricks."

I couldn't be hearing what I was hearing. It had to be a mistake. I'd learned in class that the cascade of processing sound is complex and sometimes the brain makes mistakes. "I don't understand," I whispered.

Julian dropped to his knees on the floor next to me, understanding that something was wrong but not sure what. I stared into his eyes, willing him to tell me it was a trick.

"Norman died his first month of school, Alex. He went to a party and drank too much and did drugs then passed out in a bedroom. They didn't find him til the next morning, and it was too late. He died sometime in the night." He'd said it so abruptly and without emotion that it didn't feel real. But, looking back on it now, I understand why. To him, it was a fact that was 10 months old. He'd buried his son and probably told the story hundreds of times.

But, to me, the news was minutes old. It was new information, and I had to go through the grieving process months after everyone else. I'd never get to go to the funeral or have a final good bye. My parents had taken that from me by not telling me. They'd known the school's number and could have called to get the message to me. They knew my address and could have written me or driven out to tell me. But, they'd said nothing. They'd punished me for going away to school by not telling me my oldest friend had died alone in a stranger's room hours from home. I could picture my mother weeping over his casket to make it all about her and telling everyone that I knew but chose to not come home.

"Alex?" he asked from miles away. "Are you okay?"

"No," I whispered.

"Are you alone?" he asked, and I knew he'd jump in his car and drive to me if I let him.

I continued looking into Julian's eyes, using his gaze as an anchor. I knew he knew what was happening and could hear what I was hearing in my thoughts if not from the phone itself. "No," I answered.

"Can I have your address?" he asked. "I won't give it to anyone else, but I have something that I think Norman would want you to have."

I asked Julian the question without saying it out loud. He nodded. "Sure," I said and gave the address to Mr. Crawford. The last thing he said to me was, "I'm so sorry, Alex."

When I hung up, I somehow knew it was that last time I'd ever talk to him. It was too painful for either of us to ever talk again. I would always remind him of the boy he'd lost, and he'd remind me of the friend I'd let down.

Letting the phone slide from my useless fingers, it hit the ground and was pulled into the wall by the cord. Without needing to say a word,

Julian wrapped his arms around me and let me collapse into him. The beautiful numbness was giving way to the cascading pain. The strength of the agony was more than I could hold; it burst from me in wails. Julian tried to hold me while my body shook with a grief that wanted to consume me. Zeus didn't know what to do but knew I needed him, so he rubbed his face against me, squashed between the two of us.

For what felt like hours, the three of us rocked in a mass on the kitchen floor, the cat and the vampire trying to console the broken human in a state that neither of them fully understood. When I had no more to give, when my body threatened to give out from the weight of my sorrow, Julian pulled me into him, lifted me from the ground and carried me to my bed. He lay me down, calling Zeus to join me. Rolling to my side, I faced the wall, willing all of this to be a dream but knowing it was a reality I would need to start accepting to be able to move on. Zeus jumped to lay against my chest, Julian pressed against my back.

That is how I finally fell into blessed sleep, sandwiched between two things that would fight to protect me while I fought through the next few hours of sleep, wakefulness, despair and sleep again.

The following 24 hours were like an acid trip, or so I assume that's what it was like. I'd have vivid dreams of Norman drowning in the middle of a huge lake and screaming for my help while I looked for a way to get to him. I'd wake violently, calling out into the room for my friend, only to remember he was dead and start to cry again. Then, I'd slip into sleep from sheer fatigue only to face another dream where I couldn't stop my friend from dying.

When I woke to Julian calling my name, I saw him standing next to my bed, looking down at me. "I know you're in pain," he spoke with a sternness that cut through my haze. "But you're getting up and getting into the shower. It's already running, and you smell."

I let him lift me up by my arms to standing and push me towards the bathroom. He wasn't lying, the room was full of steam and the shower pounded against the tub floor. A fresh towel and clean pajama pants sat on the closed toilet lid.

"Get in there or I will wash you myself." He meant it so I weighed my options and reluctantly did as I was told.

Fifteen minutes later, I found him in the kitchen. To my shock, he'd managed to turn on and use the oven for, what I'm sure, was the first time. He was pulling a sheet out of it with a TV dinner on top. Whatever it was, the odor hit my nose, and I was suddenly famished. At the kitchen table was a plate, silverware and a glass of water. Zeus sat in the corner, willing me to sit and eat.

The water was amazing on my ragged throat. With the number of tears that had poured out of me in the previous day, I knew I must be dehydrated. I stood to refill the glass, but Julian pushed me back into the seat. He dropped the TV dinner on my plate and grabbed the water glass to refill it. "Eat," he demanded. "I don't know how I would explain a human who starved to death in my home. Do it for me."

Pulling off the steamed plastic wrap, I saw Salsbury steak, macaroni and cheese and some green beans. It took me only minutes to devour the whole thing. I washed it all down with two more glasses of water and had to admit, I felt a little closer to myself. Julian sat at the table with me, watching me closely for signs that I may fall apart again but I didn't.

"I didn't know what you'd want so I just picked something. I don't know how many of those you are supposed to have. Do you need more?" he asked.

"Let me digest this first and I'll let you know," I answered.

"Okay," he nodded. "Perhaps," he started, scooting his chair closer to mine. "It would help to tell me about this friend that you lost." I thought about it and decided it wouldn't hurt. I might feel good to know one more person knew about Norman. It would be like he lived on. So that's what I did. For hours, I told Julian about my childhood friend. I started with the day I met him and ended with the day he dropped me off. We moved from the kitchen to the living room and then finally my room. As I crawled back into bed, I told him about my plans to talk to Norman that first week of school but forgetting, not knowing my chance was gone forever. I admitted to Julian that I wondered if me not calling him somehow contributed to him dying at that party, like he overdosed because his friend had forgotten him, but

I knew that it wasn't true. Logically, I knew that I didn't play a part in his death but needed to confess those thoughts to someone. Julian pulled the blanket over me and shook his head.

"Alex, I have been here a long time. I've seen many people die. One thing I've learned is that what is meant to happen will happen. No human, animal or vampire can stop it."

He left me with that piece of wisdom, and I believed it, believed him, and that comforted me.

The next day, I visited Isaac and Hazel. I told them, too, about my friend Norman, keeping his spirit alive through stories. They laughed with me and cried with me. It felt healing to know that three people who didn't know Norman a few days ago, now knew him.

As days passed, I was starting to return to a new kind of normal. I'd managed to get back to the gym, even though it reminded me of Norman's garage gym. I'd returned to classes, and was feeling less guilty for being able to go to class when Norman never would again. I ate, I showered, I hung out with friends and played with Zeus.

So, the large package showing up at the door, worried me. I knew it was from Mr. Crawford and stared at it like it was a coiled snake, ready to bite. Whatever was in there could either help me through the next stage of grieving or send me backwards into a quivering pile. I didn't know what it would be until I opened it.

I waited for Julian to rise for the night and asked him to open it in the next room, away from me. Then, he could use his judgement to decide if I should see it or he should burn it. Unfortunately, the plan fell apart when Julian called from the living room, "I'm not even sure what it is, Alex." So, I was forced to see it myself. Relief and laughter burst out of me when I saw Julian turn and reveal the mystery gift.

Norman's skateboard, with his Sharpie spider drawn across the bottom, was gripped in the hands of a confused vampire and it was the best thing I'd ever seen.

Fall semester of our sophomore year was like a new chapter for me. Norman's skateboard was hung on the wall of my bedroom, reminding me that no day is promised, and every morning is a gift. A bounce was in my step as I walked into the cafeteria to see Isaac and Hazel at our usual table. Cohabitating had put a glow in their cheeks. We compared schedules to see if we had any overlap but each of us were getting deeper into our chosen majors and none of our classes were the same. Hazel's schedule was heavy in psych and counseling, Isaac was all music, and I was straight pre-med. We promised to continue our breakfast and lunch routine so we wouldn't lose touch, then went our separate ways.

By lunch, we each had the stare of a student who has just realized the easy days of freshmen year were behind us. "I'm going to have to study 20 hours a day," Hazel sighed.

"Same," I commiserated.

"Maybe we could drop out and live in a van by a beach and grow our own food or something," Isaac offered, and I made us laugh, as I think he intended.

Hazel turned to me, "Excited to play tonight?" she asked.

"Yeah," I said. "It'll be a good escape to be Ajax again. I miss him."

"Is Julian coming," she asked, and I could tell she wanted to ask more but didn't.

"Yeah, why?"

"Just wondering," she smiled. "How are you two getting along? Living together can be stressful."

I looked at Isaac. Was something wrong between them? Was moving in together putting a rift in their relationship. "It's fine, why? Are you guys good?"

"Yes," Isaac said and laid his hand on Hazel's. "We're good and we're happy for you and it's none of our business. Right, Hazel?"

Now, I was confused. "What's not your business?"

"Are you gay?" Hazel asked.

Isaac rolled his eyes, threw his head back and covered his face with his hands. "Hazel," he exclaimed through his hands. "Why?" He pulled his hands down and looked at her. "We had a whole talk about this." Then, he looked to me. "Alex. I'm sorry. It's not our business and we don't care, man. We love you no matter what."

Frozen, a spoonful of mashed potatoes halfway to its destination, my mouth dropped open. "What are you talking about?"

Hazel answered. "You and Julian. You told us he was gay and now you guys live together and honestly, you're both gorgeous, so it makes sense."

Laying my potatoes back on the plate, I gulped down water then locked eyes with Hazel. "I am not gay," I insisted.

"You're not?" She asked.

"No," I answered.

"But," she side-eyed Isaac whose eyes were clearly tell her to stop but she ignored him. "You didn't hook up at all last year. I mean, are you a virgin?"

"No," I responded too quickly. And this one gave me pause. I had to think for a minute. I mean, I'd been with one girl, and it was over before

I knew what happened. And while, yes, it was good, I'd made myself feel the same way with masturbation, so I just didn't get the appeal of sex.

"You're not answering," she prodded.

"Well," I decided to just be honest. "I've only been with one. And, it wasn't as good as everyone says so I don't see the point."

"Alex," Isaac leaned in. "Maybe you just haven't been with the right person. I mean, it's like pizza, it can be amazing, or it can just be okay. Depends on who you get it from."

Hazel slapped his arm. "Really? Pizza?"

He kissed her cheek. "Yeah, and yours is the best." Her fake indignation faded, and she was back to glowing.

She turned back to me. "We were both with people before each other. You kind of have to. That's how you figure out what you like. Isn't that what college is about, getting to know yourself? And, trust me, half these girls would fight each other to spend a night with you."

Hazel had a point. Was I missing out by not having unattached flings with co-eds? Just because I had a serious goal didn't mean I couldn't have some fun. And, maybe it would help me relax which would then help me focus on schoolwork.

I made it my mission for sophomore year to explore my sexuality and figure out what all the hype was.

24

At the risk of angering those who are reading, I won't go into vivid details about my sophomore escapades. Sadly, it's not worthy of taking up paper space, but I'll give a brief overview of the year.

We played Raven Realm three nights a week like always. Several new students joined up and we elected Tony as the new game master since Drew had graduated. He was creative with his story lines, taking turns giving all of us a chance to be main characters.

Even though I knew Julian was in the group because he had to be, he couldn't hide how much fun he had. The new girls were madly in love with him, but he kept up the façade of being homosexual to deter their crushes. I'd been very candid with him about my lack of experience, and he was surprisingly supportive with my quest. Sometimes I'd forget how old he was and then he'd say something like "I have had more dalliances than I can recollect," and I'd remember. He'd described sex as an "elevated experience" and I wanted to have what he described.

It was one of the new girls in our group that I first slept with that year. Her name was Mary, and she was majoring in finance. Her hair was true red, and I'd thought she was beautiful. One night, after group, she'd asked if I wanted to look at stars and I'd agreed, letting her lead me into the woods and then into a clearing. She's pulled a bottle of vodka out of her bag, and we'd taken turns gulping down the burning liquid until we'd drowned our inhibitions and given into our instincts. She'd taken the lead, much like my first time. But this time she'd told me what she wanted, and I'd followed instructions. It had given me a little more control in the moment, a little more knowledge of women's desires and it'd felt good to do more than just lay there. Still, when it was done, I'd recognized it felt good but didn't think it was the explosive experience I'd heard others describe. And, to my surprise, she didn't want more and was fine with just having sex. We'd do it several more times before she would tell me she had a boyfriend and was done with our trysts.

Natalie had been a month or so later. She was a chemistry major, so we'd crossed paths before in the science building. I'd asked her if she wanted to study together, and she'd smiled. "I'm in the C building, room 430. My roommate is gone this weekend if you want to study."

We hadn't even started to pull out books to keep up the appearances of studying. As soon as I was in her room, she'd pulled off her shirt, was dropping to her knees and pulling at my jeans. What we did that night was frenzied and like people starved for something. It served its purpose and we both found release but, again, I didn't feel the "spark" that so many people describe. Her and I never really spoke again so I guess I wasn't the right fit for her either.

There was a girl who wanted to tie me up, which I declined and excused myself. There was a girl who insisted on leaving the lights off and only wanted missionary, which is fine but felt more like going through the motions than having real fun. After that, I took a break from trying to find my "sexual self" and re-focused on the gym. If I'm being honest, I found more joy in lifting weights than sleeping with women. Julian, Isaac and Hazel all told me the same thing, that I just needed to find the "right one."

In May, as the year was coming to an end, I thought they may be right and tried my luck with a girl from the gym. We we're both fit and

I felt a little chemistry when we talked so decided to ask her on a date. After dinner, we went back to her room. By then, I'd learned enough to please women and my time with her felt more pleasurable than the other times had been. When it was over, she explained that she wasn't looking for anything serious and didn't want more than that night. Truthfully, as the excitement of the moment wore off, I was relieved it would only be once.

Walking back home, I started to accept that something was wrong with me, and I just wasn't meant to be sexual or in a relationship. If I was honest with myself, I got more enjoyment out of fitness, studying and taking steps towards helping people than I did from sex. I decided I was done with girls while in college. Maybe, once in med school or practicing as a doctor, I'd try again. Or, perhaps, after I'd created the cure, I could focus more on my human needs. But, for the moment, I just wanted to spend time with my friends and work on my goals.

Climbing up the steps, I didn't think much about the cracked open front door. Sometimes, especially on the nice nights, Julian would crack the door when he woke to let Zeus wonder outside. The cat didn't go far; he was spoiled and loved to hang out with us more than he liked to explore. In fact, he was in his favorite outdoor spot, lying on the porch chair and watching a bird hop through a tree.

"Hi, buddy," I said. He rolled to his back to show me his tummy, and I obliged by scratching it. When I stopped, he jumped down and I knew he'd follow me inside to get more scratches or try to convince me Julian didn't already feed him. Instead, he stopped at the open door and turned to return to his chair, leaving me to enter alone.

"There he is," I heard before I was fully inside and turned to face the living room full of people. No, that's not accurate - the room full of vampires.

25

Julian stood in front of the fireplace, looking like a child who'd been caught with his hand in the cookie jar before dinner. On the couch sat three vampires, all of them unmoving in a way that no human could manage. There wasn't a single twitch, sniffle, adjustment or cock of the head. They just stared at me. Each set of eyes shone inhumanly and, not for the first or last time, I wondered how other humans couldn't see it. Two women and a man stood in tandem. I braced myself for attack, but the man gestured for me to sit in the chair facing the couch. Heart pounding in my ears, I kicked off my shoes and crossed to sit. Once I did, they also sat.

"You are Alex?" The blonde woman asked, and I nodded.

"Are you fully human?" The black-haired woman asked. I nodded.

"You don't feel entirely human," the man stated. I looked to Julian, but he'd fixed his expression to show nothing.

"I don't know what you mean," I didn't know if any of them could read minds, so I didn't bother to lie. It was a good thing because the second woman turned to the first and said "He really doesn't."

The first woman arched an eyebrow. "Curious," she said, then stood. When she crossed to me and reached out a hand, I couldn't stop myself from flinching. She couldn't have been more than five feet tall, but I was terrified. "I don't plan to hurt you," she said, and I believed her. "I'm Zora." I took her hand, and she didn't move to shake it or squeeze it.

"Kiss it," Julian guided, and I did. He took a step towards us. "This is the Lady of the city," he explained.

She turned to him, and he froze. "Does he know what that means? How many of our secrets have you shared, Julian?"

He returned to his spot in front of the fireplace, eyes down. "He knows only that you are in charge and asked me to watch the LARP group. That is all."

The black-haired woman spoke without being asked. "He tells the truth."

Zora smiled. "Thank you, Jeannette." She slid her hand from mine and slowly made her way to Julian who continued to gaze at his feet. "So, you move a human in and tell him about vampires? What should we do with you?"

I jumped to my feet. "He didn't tell me. I already knew." She whirled to face me. Everything within me screamed to flee yet I knew it would be the worst thing I could do. Instinct told me that backing down or showing weakness would be like spilling blood into a shiver of sharks.

"How?" Zora asked.

Again, it was pointless to lie. "My sister is a vampire."

"Her name?" she asked.

"Sheena," I answered. "She was turned in 1988. I don't know by who or where she is."

Jeannette stood, moved to me in a way that looked like floating and stared into my eyes. Her irises were a brown that leaned closer to yellow than brown. They were the eyes of a predator. It was hard to hold their gaze as she searched for something in mine. When she moved to Zora and whispered in her ear, I saw intrigue in the Lady's response. Jeannette returned to the couch to sit. Zora glided silently to stand in front of me and amusement had replaced the anger that was boiling only seconds prior. "So, you think you can make vampires human again?"

"Possibly," I choked out through my fear.

The male vampire on the couch jumped to his feet. "Heresy," he cried out.

Zora barked at the man but kept her eyes on me. "Calm yourself, Byron." And he sat back down like a well-trained dog.

"Why should I allow you to live?" She asked with the same urgency as someone asking about a restaurant's specials. "A human who knows of our kind is dangerous," she looked to Julian for the next line. "That's why we swear to secrecy and don't live with them." She turned back to me. "And, one that wants to experiment with our very existence." She laid a chilly hand against my cheek. "That feels risky."

I couldn't stop myself from trembling and my legs threaten to give way at any moment. "Yet," she ran her hand down to my chest. "Advances in society do not come without risk. And, I think there is merit to being able to undo the turn." My heart rate slowed a little as I understood she wasn't completely against my plan. "What a punishment it could be to errant vampires, making them human again." Never mind, I didn't like where this was headed but didn't want Jeannette to read my thoughts so forced myself to smile as Zora trailed her hand across my pecs and down my arm. "You all are so vulnerable and easy to kill." She stopped just before she reached my hand, wrapping her grip around my wrist and squeezing. "What a threat it would be to those who don't obey me to lose their immortality and strength."

The certainty that she would break my wrist to make her point came to me only a moment before she did that very thing. The cracking of my bones hit my ears first, then the searing pain was next. I dropped to the ground, cradling my hand against my chest and fighting the urge to whimper. Julian moved towards me again, but I saw his feet freeze mid-step. Zora words hit me like actual flame too close to my skin. "That is what happens when you bring a human into our world without securing my permission and protection first. You're lucky that is all I did."

When she spoke again, her voice felt like the caress of satin down my body. "Stand up, Alex." I did as I was told, feeling the world swim around me for a terrifying few seconds then my view refocused on her in front of me. She rose up on her tiptoes to lay a soft kiss on my pounding jugular. "I'm sorry I needed to do that but I need for you to understand how quickly I can hurt you for the next thing. But first, Byron, heal the boy."

I didn't know what was going on and didn't want any more vampires touching me. Involuntarily, I dropped backwards to sit in the chair, trying to get away from Byron as Zora returned to the couch and he approached me. Light glinted off the knife he pulled from behind his back, placed against his forearm and slid across this forearm. Shoving the wound in my face, I pulled back. "It'll heal you. You got 30 seconds before the wound closes so drink fast; I won't do it twice." I looked to Julian who nodded.

"I'll be a vampire," I gasped.

"No, you won't," Julian insisted.

I didn't know if I could trust anyone in that moment. The pain screaming in my arm was threatening to knock me out. I watched as the slice on Byron's arm started to close and knew I needed to choose quickly. When I locked my mouth over his wound and sucked, I was telling myself that if I became a vampire, I could just cure myself later but hoped that was not my outcome.

I could only manage a single gulp when the slice stopped producing blood. Pulling back, I saw a pristine forearm with no sign of damage. "Incredible," I said, looking up to Byron who was smiling at me like I was a silly child. He returned to the couch without a word, sitting down.

"By tomorrow morning," Zora lectured. "You'll be back to your usual." She leaned forward. "Remember, as you heal, that I *allowed* you to be healed. I am being kind to you for three reasons. First, you didn't know better. Second, because you didn't lie once this night and that is rare. Third," the smile that crossed her face filled my veins with ice water. "I think we can use you."

Without word, all three stood and crossed to the front door. Julian moved to see them out and I followed out of a mix of fear and relief they were leaving. While we stood on the porch, Jeannette and Byron descended to the car that I hadn't noticed when I'd come home. Zora stayed behind to talk to us. I think she wanted only us to hear her next words because she spoke in a whisper. "You will tell me every step you take towards the cure. When you find it, you tell only me. Do you understand?"

"Yes," I manage with shaky breath.

As they drove away, I knew I was in deep but wasn't even close to understanding how bad an alliance with Zora was.

26

As soon as we were inside, I retreated to my bedroom and the false security of being under a blanket. The half-decent sex I'd started the night with felt like it had happened a week prior, and I'd lived a lifetime since. My wrist throbbed. I worried that they'd lied about the healing, that they were screwing with the human, and I'd need to go to the ER in the morning. Zeus jumped up and curled himself into a fluffy ball between my legs. I was sitting in my bed, so he'd be mad when I needed to lay down but, for now, I let him enjoy his rest.

Julian entered with a bottle of Tylenol and a glass of water, a peace offering. He stood at the side of my bed. "Can you forgive me?" he asked, extending his arms to show me his gift of analgesia.

I took it. "You didn't do it."

"I knew the danger of allowing you in," he sat on the floor, watching me swallow the pills and wash them down. "Yet, I did it. Selfishly, because I didn't want to be alone anymore."

I let that roll through my brain, understanding why he'd made the choice to trust me. I'd also felt alone so much of my life, like I didn't really fit in with everyone around me. I didn't have many people in my life that I truly cared about; I'd lost Norman and Sheena. I couldn't fathom how many people Julian had lost.

"It's okay," I said. "At least, she only punished me."

His eyes dropped to the ground. "I was punished before you came. They were here for a while."

I didn't know what his punishment had been and didn't want to push. He'd share if he wanted to or was allowed to. For now, I just wanted him to stop feeling bad. "When did you get Tylenol?" I asked.

He laughed. "When you agreed to move in. I know you can be hurt so I got everything in the first aid aisle. It's all in a box under the sink if you need it."

"It feels a little better already," I said and wasn't lying. "Did they tell the truth?" I was afraid to ask but I had to know. "Will I be healed and not turn into a vampire?"

He looked back up at me, sincerity in his eyes. "Yes," he said. "It's true. You have to be emptied of blood and then drink ours to turn. And ingesting a small amount of our blood will heal but only small injuries, Alex." He took in a deep breath and let it out. "And, she was being truthful about the rarity of her kindness. She must like you to inflict such little damage only to heal you immediately."

"I see," but did I really? Did I know what tonight had meant? "Am I in danger?"

"I want to tell you no," he admitted. "I want to tell you I can protect you."

"But?" I urged.

"But," he sighed. "I am not strong among my kind and I'm young. I stay to myself for a reason, so I don't piss them off. It's best to stay under the radar. And, after tonight, we're not only on the radar but in her sights. She won't stop until she has what she wants."

"What if we can't do it? What if I don't find the cure?"

He shook his head. "I don't want to know, Alex. I think it's best we do what we planned and take it step by step, letting her know what those steps are and that we are working on it. She knows that it will be a decade and a half before you can even start your work but 15 years to her is nothing." He stood and picked up Zeus. I think he was using the cat to comfort him. "We've bought ourselves some time. Let's just focus on that. I'll take charge of giving her updates. You don't need to talk to her again."

"Okay," it gave me some comfort. "We continue as planned; nothing has changed."

But that was a lie, everything had changed.

27

Zora was content to let Julian be our mouthpiece. Throughout junior year, she'd randomly show up on campus. I'd be walking out of dinner to see her on the quad, beckoning me over to her, Jeannette always at her side. She'd interrogate me about if I'd learned anything to help with the cure, if I'd told anyone or if I'd seen my sister. Each time, I'd answer, and her sidekick would assure her I was honest. A few times, Isaac or Hazel would see the strange woman beckoning me over and ask who she was. I'd beg them to please drop it.

Once, I'd tried to explain to Zora that I needed to go to medical school, complete years of residency and specialize in hematology before I could even begin to start to design the study. I tried to make them understand that it could take years of testing, study and experimentation to even crack the code to understand vampirism as a condition. Each time I tried to explain, Zora would wave her hand at me like I didn't know what I was talking about.

By the end of the year, I was terrified every time the sun went down that this was the night Zora would have hit the end of her patience and snap my neck in a rage.

Julian insisted he'd gone to her and tried to explain the same thing only to be thrown against a wall and told to come to her only when asked.

We were between a rock and an impatient vampire master. The best thing we could do was make sure we stayed quiet and responded when addressed.

We'd stopped playing Raven Realm. She'd told Julian there was no need to anymore, saying she'd sent another vampire to play and wanted him to put his energy into getting into med school. I didn't see the joy in playing anymore. Now that I really knew what vampires were like, I didn't want to pretend anymore. Every time Tony would talk about the "dangers of the Dark," I'd feel a roll of nausea and want to say "You have no idea what you're talking about." Finally, I'd just stopped going.

It was the last night of the semester, when Hazel and Isaac found me sitting alone in the library and confronted me about my strange behavior. They sat down on each side of me; Isaac's voice startled me out of my reading. "What's going on, Alex?"

I shut the book and looked up. "What do you mean?"

Hazel grabbed my arm, so I'd turn to her. "You're acting so weird. We're worried about you. You look terrible, you quit the game, and you never come over anymore. You barely eat or talk."

Isaac picked up where she left off. "Whatever it is, man. You can tell us. We can help."

"No, you can't," I blurted out before I could stop myself. I didn't say anything else but that one sentence told that they were right; something was going on and I was hiding it.

"What's going on, Alex?" Hazel persisted.

"Yes, what is going on, Alex?" I shot up, facing the voice. Zora and Jeannette stood in the stacks to the right of our table. I hadn't heard them approach. The vampires slunk towards us, and I instinctually moved to stand between them and the table with my friends. They stopped, laughing at the idea that I could do anything to stop them. "Introduce us to your companions, Alex," Jeannette purred. "They are obviously very important to you."

"Are they?" Zora asked. "How important?"

"Very," Jeannette answered. I shivered, knowing there was nothing I could do if the vampires wanted to hurt us. They could slaughter us all, remove the bodies, clean the mess and wipe the librarian of any memory we'd ever been here.

Hazel stood and came around me to extend her hand. "I'm Hazel and this is my boyfriend, Isaac."

Something slid over Zora's face, and she suddenly appeared to be a happy, college co-ed. All signs of her age, power and otherworldliness were gone. If I didn't know better, I would have thought she wasn't old enough to drink and was as naïve as a child. "Hi," she beamed. "I'm Zora and this is my girlfriend, Jeannette." Hazel shook each vampire's hand, Isaac stood to do the same and again I wondered how my friends couldn't see that they weren't human.

Jeannette and Zora leaned in tandem, one catching Hazel's eyes and the other catching Isaac's. Together they spoke, "Tell Alex good night, go home, sleep well and only remember meeting two nice girls."

My friends turned to me, bid me good night and started to walk out. Relief washed over me but was replaced with horror when Zora spoke. "Oh, Isaac? Where do you live again."

Isaac turned, gave his full address and then I watched them leave. Trembling I faced the vampires. All pretense of sweet humanity was gone again. "Why?" I asked.

"To keep you in line," Zora said plainly.

"Don't hurt them," I begged.

"Don't make me," she quipped and then they were gone.

28

The summer before my senior year brought acceptance letters, and scholarships, to every medical school I'd applied to. Whenever I saw the Lady Zora, I'd tell her about each one. At first, she was pleased but quickly realized me going to med school didn't quicken the timeline, it was just the next step. Once I explained to her that some were on the other side of the county, she'd delivered the edict that I was to stay within a 100-mile radius of her territory, and I agreed. I wasn't ready to tell her that my residency was not up to me and where I matched, I would have to go. It could very well be on the west coast. Once I specialized, it would be even harder to control my destination. But I figured I would cross that bloody bridge once I got there.

Once the school was chosen and I'd notified them, we got to work on getting Julian accepted as well. We had a year to prepare, but we'd need to find a place to live, ensure it was set up for him, get the approval of whatever vampire was in charge of that area and make sure Zora was happy.

Moving is so much more complicated for a vampire than humans realize.

A couple of days before our last year at the same college, Isaac asked me to meet him for dinner, and it hit me that moving meant saying goodbye to my friends as well. When I saw him at the restaurant, I was surprised Hazel wasn't there. He stood as I approached the table, and we hugged. "Where's your better half?" I asked.

"She went home for the week," he sat. "It's time for her to get all her stuff and just be done with them. She's seeing her little sister's high school graduation and then I don't think she'll ever go back again."

"Is that a good thing?" I remembered what Hazel had told me about her home life and growing up but didn't want to assume.

"A very good thing," he answered. "I mean I know I'm lucky with my family, but I support cutting off people that hurt you, no matter who they are. Movies are always telling you that love is unconditional and how love means not saying sorry and you should fight for love. It makes people feel like you have to stick it out no matter what or it's not love." He leaned in. "But I think that's bullshit. The words mean nothing, man. It's all about action. If someone treats you bad, they don't love you and you don't owe them anything."

While he looked over his menu, I processed what he said. Without knowing it, he'd taken the years of guilt I'd felt for cutting off my parents and just washed it all away. He was right. I didn't owe them anything and they'd never really loved me. So, why should I feel ashamed for not loving them in return?

He laid down his menu. "So, she's saying her goodbyes, walking away and never looking back. Only ahead. "

"And then what?" I asked.

"We're both going to stay for grad school. We both got accepted. We want to do like a counseling program. She does the talk therapy, and I can do the music therapy. Maybe we can open like a community center and help all these people who have been through the kind of stuff you and her have."

My heart pinged when I thought that I may have helped these two come together and inspired even a part of what they wanted to combat all the suffering this world offered. I had a vivid image of the two of them in a classroom, singing and clapping in front of a room of kids. Isaac happily played the guitar while Hazel led the kids in a rendition of some silly song.

The waiter took our orders while we talked about how far we'd all come since the first day of freshman year in the school cafeteria. Who could have foreseen the moment we found ourselves in, with our paths so open and promising?

"So," Isaac spoke around a mouthful of pasta. "Ready for med school?"

I stabbed a meatball with my fork and really thought about it. "I don't know, man. I mean, it's kind of huge and it was always the plan. But, it's scary as hell."

"Yeah, it's gonna be intense but if anyone can do it, it's you."

"I kind of have to." I let that hang in the air, knowing he'd think it was just me being committed to being a doctor when I knew I really did have no choice anymore. If I didn't go to med school, a crazy vampire would probably show up at Isaac's house and wipe with the floor with him to make a point.

"I get that," he said. "I'm glad you'll have Julian. I'll just miss you and you being down the street."

"Yeah," I didn't want to think about it. "I will too. But we'll talk every week on the phone, and I'll come to visit during breaks."

"I just hope you'll come home for the wedding."

I dropped my fork and stared. He smiled, pulling a small black box from his pants' pocket. I didn't need him to open it to know what was inside. But, seeing the little ring did drive it home. "Holy shit, dude. Seriously?"

"Yeah," he beamed. "I'm asking her once she's back. I want to help her unload everything and really process but then, when the moment is right, I'm asking her."

"Congratulations, Isaac. I couldn't be happier for you guys."

"You'll be my best man, of course?"

"Of course," I clapped. Waving the waiter over, "Champagne please. We're celebrating."

"You might want to wait for her to say yes first."

"She'll say yes," I assured him. "I've seen you two together."

When the bubbling golden liquid was poured, we toasted to them, to happiness, to friendship, to love and to the future.

It felt like everything was going to be okay.

29

The first day of senior year, I made my way to the cafeteria and was disappointed to not see Isaac and Hazel there. It occurred to me that we hadn't compared our schedule for this year, and it was possible that they both had early classes, or both had decided to sleep in due to later classes. My schedule was packed, and I wouldn't be surprised if theirs were too.

I missed lunch, choosing to grab a protein bar and hit the gym instead.

When they didn't show up to dinner either, I knew something was wrong. It hadn't occurred to me that Hazel might have said no to the proposal but maybe she had. Maybe they were trying to work through it. Or, maybe, she'd said yes, and they were entwined in newly-engaged bliss.

The empty table the next morning was the moment I decided it was time to go visit them. If I interrupted some kind of engagement sex-fest, so be in. But I didn't want to not check on them and something was wrong.

Once my classes wrapped for the day, I started the walk to their apartment building. When I didn't see their car, I worried I'd walked all the way for nothing. But they did share one car, so it was possible one was home and the other wasn't. Since I was there, I'd might as well knock.

No answer came and I almost walked away but something inside me was screaming that something was wrong. I didn't see anything to raise that suspicion, but I just knew, deep down, that something was off. When I tested the door, it was unlocked so I made the decision to just go in.

Darkness made it hard to navigate the first room. I paused and called out. "Guys? Anyone home? It's Alex."

Silence was my only answer, so I knew I'd come over and entered my friends' apartment for nothing, but I was also relieved I hadn't walked in on them being intimate. I headed towards the kitchen, feeling around on the wall for the light switch. I had a plan to find a pen and paper, leave a message, then head home when a whimper hit my ears.

Flipping on the light, I followed the sound into the hallway and down to the bedroom. Lightly I tapped a knuckle against the door. Only then, just before the moment I swung the door open, did it occur to me that Zora may be here. If she'd done something to them because I'd brought her to them, I'd never forgive myself.

I hesitated, wondering if I should go get Julian, and worried I was about to see something I could never unsee. But, if they were hurt, I had to help them.

My eyes had to adjust to the darkness of the room. It was obvious someone was in the bed; the mounded shape was human-like. But I didn't know if it was male, female or alive. I took a cautious step into the room, hearing the whimpering again.

"Hello?" I asked.

A wail hit my ears and the agony in it broke my heart. It was the sound of pure human suffering, a sound everyone can recognize. It brought a visceral reaction from me, a fear of what caused that suffering but also a guttural desire to help the creator of that sound. I lurched forward, dropping onto the bed to touch the blanketed lump. My chest was tight; I couldn't breathe until I knew who this was and what was wrong.

Once my hand was on the form, I registered it was male, and it was warm, so Isaac was alive at least. "Isaac?" My voice shook.

He rolled over to look at me. My relief that he was alive was washed away by the sight of him. His eyes were swollen from crying, the whites of them marbled by redness. "What's wrong?" I asked. "Did someone hurt you?"

"Hazel," he whispered, and I saw he was clutching his fist to his chest. "Hazel."

"Hazel, what?" I asked, afraid to hear the answer. "Where is she? Did someone take her?"

"No," he shook his head. His mouth opened and shut over and over like he wanted to say something but couldn't.

"No, no one took her? Where is she? Is she coming back."

"No," he managed. "She's home."

"What do you mean she's home? She's still with her family?" But that didn't make sense. He wouldn't be this upset if she was with her family. He reached the clutched fist towards me, unfurling it to show a piece of paper inside. I took it. As I opened the crumbled ball, he sat up, turning to place his feet on the ground then remained seated on the edge of the bed, back to me, like he couldn't face what I was about to do.

The sheet of notebook paper had started life as a simple piece of school supplies. When I flattened it out, I read the scribbled words aloud. "Car accident. 8/24/1999. DOA. TOD 2257. Funeral 8/29 at 10am."

Staring at Isaac's back, I didn't want to believe that those words meant what they did. I didn't want to even begin the question that was brewing in my mind. He started instead, speaking to the floor in a monotone. "She was headed here, from her dad's place. Left there a day before she was supposed to. Her and her dad had fought, and she wanted to get back to me. Some man in a pickup truck was driving home from a birthday party, drunk, going too fast. He ran a stop sign and hit her car, pushed her into a lamp pole. By the time they pulled her out of our car, it was too late. There was nothing they could do."

"No," I whispered. "There must be a mistake."

He continued. "Her little sister called me. Hazel had given her our number in case she ever wanted to get away from there."

I crawled to the edge of the bed, sat next to him, afraid to touch him. It was like, if I touch him, it would remind me that we were in reality, and I'd have to face that this wasn't a dream. "How do we know? What if they're lying? Holding her there?"

The sigh that came out of him was a mix of lost hope and complete anguish. "The police called me next. The car was in my name."

"No," I whispered.

"It's real," he took away any chance of me pretending, any hope of a crazy explanation. I touched his leg, and it set off both our tears. "The funeral is in two days. I don't know if I can."

"I'll go with you," I said. To my shame, I was relieved to be able to see her one final time. Norman had been in the ground almost a year before I heard. Sheena just disappeared with no chance for closure. I couldn't bear the thought of losing another person I loved without getting to say goodbye.

30

When I'd opened the closet to help him pick something out for the funeral, we'd discovered that all the dark clothing belonged to Hazel. After half a dozen times of pulling out a black item to only be met with her smell and realize she'd never wear it again, we stopped hunting. Instead, Julian had offered one of his black suits to Isaac, along with his car for the trip.

We headed out early the day of the service. It was the usual, overcast grey of the north-east as summer gave way to fall and a four-hour drive in silence. Neither of us wanted to talk about her but neither of us wanted to talk about anything else.

Behind us, three cars followed, full of everyone from Raven Realm who remained at our school. Telling them had been difficult. I will never forget walking into the meeting room and seeing how excited they all were that I'd returned, only to see confusion on their faces when they realized I wasn't in costume. Then, the reactions of the group when I told them that our beautiful witch was gone. Iris had to be taken to the hospital to be medicinally calmed, and her parents had traveled into town to be with her for the funeral.

We'd all come to the consensus that we would not attend the service. None of us were church people and none of us wanted to be in the same room as the parents who'd been so vile to her as a child. We all had heard her stories, seen her scars, and had nothing nice to say to her mother or father. So, we'd all go to the cemetery to watch her be put to rest.

Her spot was set up with flowers, chairs and a huge picture of her on an easel making it easy to find. We'd gotten there before the service was done, so we were the first to stand at the site of her final rest, and got the alone time we needed to perform our own little funeral.

One by one, the members of Raven Realm walked up to the portrait to say their last words to her. It ranged from humorous to heartbreaking, with each Hazel memory that was shared, until Isaac and I remained.

I stepped up to the picture and let the world around me slide away. "Hazel, when I was ten, my sister was taken from me, and a piece of my heart went with her. Then, I met you and it was like I had her back. You and her would have been best friends. You and me and Isaac in the cafeteria will be my favorite memories to cherish until the end of time. I didn't know what family was supposed to be like until I found you two. I will love you forever and I promise to take care of Isaac for you. Please be at peace and watch over us if you can."

Isaac's hand on my back told me he was next to me and ready to talk. I stayed while he did. "Hazel, you are the love of my life. You brought so much into my life that I didn't know I needed. I think that you were too special to be on this Earth for any longer, you were needed somewhere else. I was so mad that you were taken away from me but now I just think of how lucky I was to have had that time with you." He pulled the ring box from his pocket and looked at it. "I wanted so badly to ask you and hear you say yes. I hate that man for taking that moment away from us." The eyes that looked from the box to her picture were filled with tears. "But I know you would have said yes, and I can hear it in my ears and close my eyes and see the moment and that will have to be enough." He turned to the rectangle pit in the ground that would house his fiancé in less than an hour, letting the box fall from his hand

and into the hole. When he looked back at Hazel, he smiled. "You should have it. It was always going to be yours. I love you."

The arrival of the hearse was our signal to move into the background. Watching the people pour from the cars, it was easy to see who the mother, father and sister were. Hazel's little sister was a younger version of her and the vacant look in her eyes was one I knew well. I only hoped she was headed off to college to escape, like her sister and I had. Hazel's father was emotionless in a way that made me hate him even more. I wanted him to be filled with regret for the way he'd treated her, shame for driving her out of his home a day early so she'd be in the path of a drunk driver, or sorrow for the lost time with his oldest child. Instead, he looked like a man annoyed by the business of funerals and having better places to be. In that moment, Hazel's father became my father and Hazel's mom became my mom. I felt my fists clench at my side, my muscles trembling to be used.

The coffin being pulled from the back of the hearse sent ice water through my rage.

I didn't hear anything the priest said as the coffin was placed over the burial site. Ringing filled my ears while women wept, and attendees crossed themselves. To my left, Iris began to cry quietly and grabbed my hand. To my right, Isaac stood frozen, only the heaving of his chest told me he was aware of what was happening.

When the coffin started to lower into the ground, Isaac slipped from my periphery. He was on his knees on the ground; a broken person being asked to make it through an impossible day. Iris turned into her father who wrapped his arms around her and walked her back to their car. As the crowd around the ceremony began to disperse, heading off to a house full of finger foods and quiet conversation, I saw Hazel's family remain.

Even as I was crossing to them, my brain was screaming at me to stop. It wasn't my place, and I knew I couldn't change the past, but I couldn't cease my motion towards them. Her father looked up at me approaching, clearly confused by me. "Are you the boyfriend?"

Fury threatened to overwhelm me. "No, I am not. I'm Alex, Hazel's friend. I-"

"I don't care who you are," he interrupted. His wife and daughter huddled together, both watching the exchange. I saw that look in their eyes, the look of people who didn't know when the next slap or outburst was coming and knew no way out. "You and the freaks my daughter associated with are not welcome here."

"Sir, I-"

"Are you deaf or stupid?" he asked. "This is my daughter's funeral, and I want you and the loser she was shacking up with to leave."

My fist connected to his jaw before I knew what I was doing. He crumbled to the ground, and I had no intention of stopping. I grabbed him by his jacket and lifted him up so he could look into my eyes. He was shaking and the smell of acrid urine hit my nostril. "Hit me." I growled. "You don't mind beating children and women." I threw him to the ground. "This is your chance," I kicked him in the ribs. "You can show everyone what a tough, scary man you are. Stand up and fight."

His wife and daughter had backed away, making no attempts to stop what they were witnessing. They'd been well trained over the years to not interfere. I felt several arms pulling at me, trying to stop what I was doing. I heard Tony telling me it was time to go. From my right, Isaac stepped into my field of vision and looked down at the cowering, urine-soaked man that should have been his father-in-law. I expect my friend to apologize to the man, help him up, show him the empathy and kindness that we all loved in Isaac. Instead, Isaac stared coldly at Hazel's trembling father. "Your daughter was the greatest person I've ever known. What you put her through, what you did to her as a child, it made her who she is." He swallowed. "Who she was. But I will never forgive you. Since she is no longer here, I will take over her hatred for you. Every day you wake, every day that you get to live when she doesn't, I want you to remember that her hatred for you is still alive. That we, her friends, know who you really are."

Isaac turned from the man and took my arm. "Let's go, Alex. He's not worth your time or energy. We said our goodbyes."

I had one last thing to say to her mother. "You should have protected your children."

31

Isaac had put his semester on hold, deciding he needed time to cope before he could focus on graduating. He'd told me that he'd admired my ability to stick it out through our grieving. I couldn't tell him that I had to graduate and go to medical school or Zora would come after him. I had to tell him that I knew Hazel would want me to keep going and that seemed to make sense to him.

Julian and I took turns checking on Isaac. For weeks, he stayed in the same pajama pants and t-shirt, lying on the couch, staring at whatever was on the TV. Didn't matter if we went at noon or midnight, you'd find him on the couch in a blanket. We'd bring food and make sure he drank water. He'd perk up when we came, ask us about what the world was doing outside his apartment. But, when it was time for us to leave, he'd lay back down and stare at the TV again.

By the first snowfall, I started to worry about him. I knew everyone grieved in a different way, but this was getting bad. He hadn't shaved since the funeral, his mail piled up on the kitchen counter, he hadn't scheduled for spring semester and his guitar case was gathering dust. Julian had taken it upon himself to collect and pay all his bills for the next year, but it wasn't going to fix the real problem. We didn't know how to help Isaac and Isaac wasn't going to help himself.

The last day of the semester, I stopped by with takeout and was determined to breakthrough to him. It was time to push him.

I heard the voice on the answering machine as I walked into his apartment. His mom was saying that they hoped he'd come home for Christmas, but they were willing to come to him if it would be easier. They loved him and just wanted to know how to help.

So do I, I thought.

"Hey, man." His head popped up to look at me over the back of the couch. He'd lost more weight, confirming my suspicion that he only ate when we brought it.

"How was the last exam?" He asked.

"Hard but I studied all the right stuff so I'm not worried," I crossed to the coffee table in front of the couch and set down the takeout bags. Picking up the remnants of the meal I'd brought him the previous day, I took it to the kitchen garbage. Red and green envelopes sat atop the mail mountain. "You got some Christmas cards," I told him, getting only a grunt in response.

When the food was out of the bag and in his hands, I sat next him, shoveling chicken lo mein into my mouth to buy myself some time. "So," I began and knew I had to do it. My friend needed me to love him enough to say the hard things. "Are you going home for the holidays?"

"Nah," he said, moving his food around the white plastic carton.

"Well, we'd love you to come over to our house for Christmas then. We can make a day out of it, you know? Get you out and have some eggnog."

"Sure," he said.

The little concession gave me the courage I needed for the next two questions. "Are you going back to school next semester?"

"I think so," he shrugged. "I'm going to meet with my advisor when he's back and see what I need to do to finish."

Hope filled my chest and relief poured over me. These were all good signs, but the last part would be the hardest. "That's awesome, man. And, I was thinking," I sucked in a big breath and let it out. "This weekend, why don't we start packing up some of her stuff. Not all of it," he wasn't falling apart or kicking me out, so I kept going. "But maybe her clothes. She loved thrift stores, and I just think she'd love other girls buying her clothes there. I can help you go through stuff and drop it off." Putting more food in my mouth, I waited for his response. I had a plan for anything that could come out of him in that moment.

"Yeah, Alex." He looked up and I saw calm resolution in that gaze. "It's time. I want to keep pictures and her CDs. But," he scooped up some noodles. "It's time for me to let some other people have that stuff. Let it go to good homes." He filled his mouth and nodded along to something in his head.

"She'd like that, you know." I encouraged him. "We could even take it to like a women's shelter."

He continued to bounce his head. "Yeah, I like that. It's the kind of thing she'd love."

I was concerned that he would change his mind once I was gone, and he started to really think of what it would mean to put her dresses and books into the car and watching it drive away. However, we spent Saturday and Sunday doing that very thing. We filled boxes and bags with outfits, books, jewelry and hair accessories. We went through her shoebox of photos, sliding them into a photo album for Isaac to keep. He set it next to her binder full of CDs and her framed photo on their dresser, like a shrine. Every hour of that activity was filled with telling stories about Hazel.

When the packing up was finished and the items were in Julian's car, we worked on the apartment itself. Mail was gone through and trashed. Surfaces were wiped down, laundry was done, dust was eliminated, and windows were cracked to let the frosty, fresh air destroy the stagnant smells of sorrow.

We said our goodbyes with promises to see him at my place the next day. When I'd dropped off all the items at the local shelter, a light snow fall began, and I looked up to see a full moon. It felt like Hazel was telling me thank you and approving of our choices.

It was fresh start for us, a closing of one chapter and opening of the next. Just in time for Christmas.

32

I spent the night getting everything ready for the next day. I'd hung three stockings across the fireplace mantle. Julian had found a Christmas tree and decorated it, then spent his time trying to keep Zeus from climbing it. I wanted so badly for Isaac to have the kind of Christmas he'd described to me every year when he'd returned from his family. When the doorbell rang the next evening, we'd had a holiday record playing and a fire roaring in the fireplace.

To my surprise, Isaac had trimmed his beard, cut his freshly washed hair back to shoulder length and even had a holiday sweater on. One hand held an overnight bag and the other held a bottle of eggnog. At his feet was a large wrapped present.

"Merry Christmas Eve," he smiled, and I was thrilled at the strength of his hug. My friend was back. He was going to be okay.

"Welcome," Julian said from behind me. "Please come in."

I snatched up the present to place under the tree, then offered to take his bag. "I'll put you in my room," I said.

"Oh no, man. I don't want to put you out. You're too big for the couch."

I laughed, "It's a pull out and don't worry. You're our guest and you're taking the bedroom." Grabbing his bag, I smacked his shoulder. "Plus, you can't see Santa."

I heard Julian offer to pour him some eggnog when I took his things back to my room and tossed his bag onto the bed. When I returned, I saw they'd poured a glass for me as well. I hated the stuff but would drink it that night to add to the cheer. We went into the living room and Julian joined us a few moments later with his own glass of red liquid. "I hope you don't mind but I'll have wine instead of nog."

"Oh, no problem. I know it's not for everyone," Isaac laughed.

"So," Julian asked. "What was Christmas Eve like for you as a child?"

Isaac leaned back. "Well, we'd each get a new set of pajamas to open. Then, we'd put them on and turn on a movie. Then, Dad would read us The Night Before Christmas. We'd put out cookies and milk for Santa and carrots for the reindeer. Then, we'd all sleep in the same room, usually my brother's." He sipped at his drink and his eyes looked a million miles away. "We'd whisper and try to stay up to see Santa's sleigh. We'd promise that the first one awake the next morning would wake us all up. Eventually, we'd fall asleep."

"Sounds wonderful," Julian smiled.

"How about you?" Isaac asked him.

"Oh," he rolled the dark liquid around in his glass and was baffled . that Isaac didn't see it wasn't wine. "We were a very simple family, didn't have much money. But Christmas was our biggest meal, and my parents would save all year for the day. We'd decorate the tree with real candles and popped corn. We'd make each other gifts and sing carols, and it was one of the few times I'd be given candy. I have fond memories."

"Wow," Isaac said. "Sounds like something from a Dicken's book."

Julian laughed. "Something like that. Alex?"

I didn't see the reason to lie to these men, especially since one would know. "Before Sheena left, she'd make sure I had a great Christmas. She'd take me outside on Christmas Eve to throw down oats for the reindeer and we'd make sure the fireplace was clean. We'd hang up our stockings and talk about all the things we'd get each other when we grew up and had money. We'd watch all the specials on TV and make these long green and red chains from construction paper to hang around the tree. Then, at night, I'd sleep in her bed, and we'd talk about where in the world we though Santa was. I realized later that she'd probably shoplifted to get things for my stocking." I gulped at the eggnog to try and clear my tightening throat. "Once she was gone, we didn't celebrate anymore. No tree, no presents, no stockings and no turkey. It was just another day."

"Well," Isaac stuck out his glass for a toast. "Here's to the shit that brought us all together." We all extended our glasses into the air and drank.

We spent hours, drinking and talking about everything. Zeus moved from lap to lap, loving all the scratches he was getting. We stoked the flames, keeping it roaring despite how warm the house was. I think we all liked the idea of a fire and carols and laughter on this night. Julian brought out chestnuts, then taught us how to actually roast them over an open fire like the song says.

I was feeling the effects of the alcohol and ready to go to bed right about the time Isaac said he was heading back to enjoy his own eggnog induced slumber. He thanked Julian for welcoming him into his home, for the wonderful night and always being nice to me. He hugged me tight, telling me how much he loved me and telling me that Hazel would be so happy he wasn't alone on Christmas. I told him I loved him too but that he was drunk and needed to call it a night. He headed down the hallway, glass still in his hand and disappeared into the bathroom.

Julian and I pulled out and readied the sofa bed to the sounds of Isaac brushing his teeth, washing his face and shutting the door to my room. "He'll be okay," Julian assured me. "His mind is at peace. He's accepted that she is gone and feels like he knows what to do next. I saw nothing but happiness in his head tonight."

"Good," I sighed. "I was so scared, Julian. I thought he'd never recover."

"I've seen so much death, Alex. Everyone handles it differently. He just needed time." Julian flipped off all the lights. "Fire?" he asked.

"Let it go," I said, climbing into the makeshift bed. "I'll fall asleep to it. And, Zeus likes it." In fact, the cat had curled up at the bottom corner of my bed, in front of the flames, and was purring

"I won't be able to see you in the morning, but I hope you two have a happy one. I'll come out later to fill your stockings and put out my gifts. Please don't wait for me to open them." Before I could tell him, he should haven't gotten us anything, he was in his room.

I let the crackling of the fire, the heat of the flames and the buzz of the alcohol pull me into a heavy sleep.

It had been the perfect night.

33

"Alex," someone screamed from the dark corners of my dreams. "Alex, wake up." My eyes snapped open, to the lack of firelight and the confusion of who was calling my name or if it had been my dream.

"Now," Julian yelled from down the hall, standing in the doorway of my bedroom.

I leapt from my bed, throwing blankets aside and running to see what had caused the distress in his voice. As I reached him, I heard what he was saying. "I was putting the gifts out and his heartbeat was so slow. Help him."

The snap of the light switch accompanied the blazing bulb illuminating the room. Isaac was unmoving in the bed, sleeping in a way that reminded me eerily of Snow White in her glass coffin. Envelopes laid in a column, down the other side of the bed, single names on each one. I saw my own and couldn't figure out what I was looking at. It wasn't until I saw the empty pill bottles on the night stand next to the empty eggnog glass that I understood.

My fingers on his jugular revealed a thready pulse, his chest rose and fell at a rate too slow to truly count and was nowhere near sufficient for oxygen. The breaths were agonal, and time was not our friend. "No," I screamed. "No." I grabbed his shoulders, shaking him. "Wake up, Isaac."

"He's dying," Julian pulled me off him. "We need to get him to the hospital."

I whipped around and grabbed his arms. "Turn him."

"What?" Julian pulled away from me. "No. You don't know what you're asking."

"Yes, I do. I can't lose another person, Julian. Please, please. I can't. You can save him."

"It is not rescue, Alex. He wants to die, and I'd be giving him the exact opposite, an eternity of suffering."

"But," I stepped into him. "You said you have to choose. Give him the choice. If he wants to, he can choose to die but if he chooses to turn, we can find the cure and save him. We just need to buy him time." I dropped to my knees. "Please, Julian."

The vampire turned away, pacing around the room. I remained where I was. I'd pleaded my case and now I need to wait for the verdict. My friend's heart was slowing every second, the breaths emitting a death rattle, but I had to wait. Julian finally stopped, looked up to the ceiling and roared with frustration but I knew I'd won my case.

He stalked to the bed. "Are you sure you want this of me? Do you know what you're asking?"

Standing, I came to his side and looked down at my motionless best friend, the man who had become my brother. "Yes."

As I watched, Julian's canines extended. He struck Isaac's neck in a blur, sinking those fangs into the limp man, knowing this may be a futile exercise as he may already be gone. I wanted to look away, but my eyes stayed locked onto the scene in front of me. Julian pulled back, smashing the drinking glass against the wall and using a shard to slice his wrist open. Isaac's lip didn't even twitch when the sanguine drops hit them. "It may be too late," Julian said, laying his wrist against the man's parted mouth. I knew the wound would close soon and we were now going to have to explain to first responders why he had blood on his mouth that wasn't his and a bite mark on his neck.

Isaac swallowed.

His hands came to Julian's arm and his throat pulled down another gulp of vampire blood.

My legs gave out and I sat onto the bed, laying a hand on Isaac's shin. "We did it. He's alive." Julian pulled his arm from Isaac and took a step back. Isaac gasped, pulling in air and sat up in the bed. He looked wildly at me, then Julian, then me. He eyes trailed down the envelopes, over to the pill bottles and back to me. Confusion raced across his wide eyes. He wiped his hand over his mouth, seeing the blood on his palm and misunderstanding quickly transitioned to fear.

"You're going to be okay," I tried to soothe him.

"We don't know that," Julian snapped. "Not yet."

"What do you mean?" Isaac asked. "What happened? Why aren't I dead?"

"So," I pulled back. "You really wanted to die? Your master plan was to leave me on Christmas to find your body in my bed, to tell your family?"

"Now isn't the time," Julian pulled me off the bed to stand behind him and stepped into the bed. "Isaac. I need to tell you a lot very quickly, so I need you to listen. If you survive the day, then we will have much more time for me to explain."

"Survive the day?" Isaac's eyebrow furrowed.

"Yes," Julian sat where I had been, making Isaac look into his eyes. "I'm a vampire and I've just drained you and given you my blood. As soon as the sun starts to rise, which is soon, you will start to turn from human to vampire."

While I watched Julian trying to convince Isaac of the reality he found himself in, I witnessed him changing. A tourmaline green began to overcome the irises. His sun spots and scars faded like someone was taking an eraser to his skin. I was glued to my spot and willed myself to remember everything so I could write it down later. Would watching the transition help my research?

"Am I high?" Isaac asked. "Am I hallucinating from the pills?"

"No," Julian answered matter of factly. "When the turn happens, it will be painful. You will feel your human body die and go into a sort of limbo. Once there, you will witness the worst that your life has handed you, then be given the choice to turn or die. It will not be obvious, this choice. It's up to you, in that moment, what you do. If you make it, and rise tonight, I will teach you everything you need to know. For now, I'll leave you to Alex to explain. I need to go to bed, I can't be awake for your turn."

He left the room without ceremony, just walked out and shut the door. I knew he was upset with me, knew he hadn't wanted to turn Isaac, but I didn't care. My friend was still with us and that was all that mattered to me in the moment. "What's he talking about Alex?"

"Vampires are real. He's one. I've known for a few years about him, but I've known about vampires since high school. Sheena didn't run away; she was turned into a vampire and now you can be one too. You just have to get through the day."

"How? What are you talking about? This is crazy!"

"I know," I assured him. "But it's real and we don't have time. Just," I sat next to him. "Just make it through, okay? Try to stay and we can talk more after."

"But I don't even know what that means."

"Neither do I, not really. But, Isaac. Do you *really* want to die?"

"I don't, Alex." He angrily ran his hands down the envelopes, sending them soaring off the bed and into the air to land around the room. "I don't know how to live without her. It hurts too bad. And, if this is real. Then, you're asking me to have this pain forever."

"It won't be forever," I grabbed his hand. "It won't. The whole reason I'm becoming a doctor is to figure out how to turn vampires back into humans so I can find my sister and do it for her. I can do it for you too. You don't have to do this forever, just until I figure that out."

He stared into my eyes, searching my gaze for lies or reassurance or hope. Whatever he found there, it made his shoulders relax. "Fine," he said. "What's next?"

"I guess we wait for it to start," I resigned. "Then I will stay with you until it's done, and you wake up a vampire."

"And if I don't?" he asked.

"Then," I stood, back to him. "You finish what you started tonight, and I bury another friend."

34

The scream that ripped out of Isaac still replays in my head some-times. He doubled over, arms wrapped around his stomach, and rolled out of the bed to land on the floor in the fetal position. I stood, looking down but having no clue what to do. I ran to Julian's room and opened the door. He was laid out on the top of the blanket, motionless. I'd never looked at him while he rested, hadn't expected him to look so like a corpse. There was no chest rise, no rolling of his eyes behind the lids, no sign that he'd been animated only moments before. He wouldn't be able to help us. We were alone.

Isaac's next scream ended in the unmistakable sound of retching.

When I returned, I saw him on all fours, vomiting out black sludge onto the floor. He heaved so violently that it looked like seizures. I was paralyzed, watching my friend pay the debt for a selfish decision I'd made. When he'd emptied himself of all his bodily contents, he crawled backwards, away from the emesis and fell to his side on the floor. Not knowing what else to do, I scooped him up and laid him back in the bed. He was stiff to the touch, like his muscles had been replaced with cement. The once sun-tanned skin had taken on the grey pallor of the dead. Before his eyes closed for the last time, he attempted to say something but couldn't. Instead, he just looked at me with a mix of cautious hope and overwhelming sadness.

I was determined to stay awake until he woke, never even hosting the idea that he may not wake. If Julian was right, those who undergo the turn get to choose. Would a man who had just attempted to take his own life only hours ago really choose to return?

I spent the first two hours scrubbing the carpet of the room. The task served to keep me busy while also ensuring that my friend would wake to no reminder of his trauma. Zeus had taken up with me as a bodyguard, lying with his body pressed to Isaac's torso, like he was trying to warm him and urge him to come back.

I made a breakfast of scrambled eggs and toast, then threw it out thirty minutes later when I couldn't force myself to even take a bite.

When the morning gave way to afternoon, it occurred to me that families across the state had already opened gifts and were enjoying a Christmas day together. Loved ones were snuggled on couches by fires, people were cooking a big dinner in their kitchens, parents were building gifted toys, and one man was waiting for his best friend to either rise as the undead or succumb to death.

The presents under the tree taunted me. Their bright wrapping felt so wrong in the bleakness of the current situation. My eyes landed on the package Isaac had brought. What does a man give to his friend when he's planning to never see him open it? I was both intrigued and horrified. My feet made their way to the tree and the gift was in my hands before I knew I was going to open it. When the wrapping was tossed aside and the brown box ripped open, I looked at the items within.

Hazel's CDs, a framed photo of the two of them, the photo of her and I under the oak tree, the dress she'd worn for Raven Realm, the photo album we'd filled over the weekend and her journal had been loving wrapped and placed under the tree like a simple present and not the painful reminders of a buried girl.

I hated Isaac in that moment, hated him.

He'd planned for me to find him deceased on this morning, read whatever bullshit letter he'd left for me, give the same bullshit letters to his loved ones, then open this gift after the coroner had taken him away. I seethed in the living room, pacing and filling with rage. How could he put me through that? How could he have made the selfish decision to plan it and act it out?

Then I remembered something Julian had told me. He'd mentioned on the previous night that Isaac had been filled with peace and happiness, that he'd known what to do next. Freezing mid-stomp, the realization overcame me. He'd been at peace because he'd made the plan to end it all. I contemplated the level of pain you had to be in to find peace in a suicide plan. The rage that had been boiling was instantly cooled by the empathy I felt for the man who laid in my bed, hopefully fighting to return to the living.

Sheena had probably felt the same level of desperation when she chosen to become a vampire and abandon me. It must've hurt her greatly to leave but it was far better than staying in our home to be a human punching bag. I'd never wanted to admit it, but I'd known that my father would have eventually killed her. She'd been so much smaller than me and I'd barely survived his wrath. And to now see what a turning vampire endured as they died, it made my heart ache for my long-lost sister. She'd been so young. Had someone been with her while she turned? Had someone held her hair as she retched and died?

Returning to the bedroom, I collected the envelopes he'd thrown to the floor. Each one held a message for someone in his life. To this day I couldn't tell you what was going through my mind when I took them to the living room, lit a fire and threw them in. As I watched the one with my name be devoured by flame, I knew that Isaac may not survive the day, and I was burning his last words to me and to his family, but I didn't care. There were no remnants of the letters when I walked into that bedroom again and started the final vigil. I sat on the floor, staring at Isaac's still body. His hair had taken on a shine that no product could give you. His skin had lost any sign of the years he'd live.

Were these good signs? Did it mean he'd wake as a vampire? Or was it just the results of Julian's blood?

For hours, I sat there, back against the dresser, eyes on my friend. I willed him to choose to return, begged him to please not choose death. When the afternoon light died and the sun started to set, the reality that he may not return overcame me and the tears finally began. Exhaustion, sorrow and approaching darkness overtook me, sending me into sleep.

35

Opening my eyes to darkness, revealed nothing of importance to me. I didn't know where I was, when it was or who was with me. Scrambling to my feet, I dove for the bed and felt only empty space.

"Isaac," I screamed. Running into the living room, I was faced by two men… no, two vampires.

"I'm here," Isaac smiled.

I simultaneously registered Julian beside him on the couch, the blood-filled glasses in each hand and the lack of fire or letter burning evidence in the fireplace. It wasn't until I'd crossed to Isaac and filled my arms with him that I could begin to believe that he'd survived and was still with us.

Julian broke my trance. "Alex, do you need a drink?"

"Yes," I managed weakly, afraid to let go of my friend but knowing I needed to sit down. When Julian went for a beverage, I took his place next to Isaac, needing to be near him. Julian didn't seem to mind as he returned with the glass of liquor, handed it to me and took the chair across from us.

"We've been talking for some time," Julian began. "I've told him the basics of what he'll need to know for the next few days. We thought it best that you sleep. You've been through so much."

The liquid was a welcoming heat on my ragged throat. At the same time, I had so much to say and wanted to say nothing at all. I just wanted to listen and process before I decided what I needed to express.

I felt like I'd aged decades in a single day.

Isaac turned to me and laid a hand on my thigh. "Alex," I didn't look at him; I couldn't yet. "Alex, I'm so sorry for what I did to you. It was horrible and I wasn't in a good head space, I'm still not. But you and Julian saved me. I'd be dead if it weren't for you. You're the best friend I've ever had, and it's horrible what I was willing to put you through. I totally understand if you need some time to forgive me."

I wouldn't have known what to say, not yet, but Julian started talking and saved me from having to talk. "Isaac. This is only the beginning. I'm thrilled you survived but this is just the first step, you understand. We will need to figure out where you will live, what you will do. We need to see what powers you gain. We need to plan how to handle your family, your education. And, we must take you to Zora."

My heart plummeted into my stomach. "Is that safe?"

"It is more dangerous to hide him, Alex. You know that."

"Wait, time out. Who is Zora?" Isaac was obviously sensing my fear and was panicking in response.

"She's the vampire in charge of our area. Her law is that I should have asked permission to turn you prior it happening. Since it was an emergency, I hope she will forgive me. But we must take you to her tomorrow night to tell her that you are now a vampire and ask that she allow you to stay."

"And if she doesn't?" I asked.

"Then, we will need to leave." He answered.

I leapt to my feet. "No," I exclaimed. "We didn't go through all of this just to be sent away."

"Alex," Julian held up his hand. "Calm yourself. Let's take this one problem at a time. Let me worry about how to handle Zora. For this night, can we just enjoy each other's company and have our Christmas?"

"I agree," Isaac joined in. "I don't know what this all means or what's going to happen, but I'd like to have a nice Christmas night before we have to face any problems."

So, that's what we did. We spent the precious pre-sunrise opening gifts, emptying stockings, laughing and enjoying our little protective bubble for the night. I was surprised by Isaac's great thirst that first night. He'd emptied half a dozen glasses of blood, which Julian assured us was normal. The elder vampire had told Isaac several times that the extreme hunger would abate, but for now he had enough to satiate the newly turned.

Throughout our time, I tried so hard to just be in the moment, be present for the precious time that we had. However, in the base of my soul, I knew that a rocky journey was ahead of us. I knew that we had to face Zora the next night. I knew that the need to find a cure was now the greatest of imperatives and solely on my shoulders.

It was a Herculean task to keep all my fears suppressed for that night, but I did, knowing that Julian could read my mind and would know my unrest.

I was too afraid to ask Isaac if he was happy that I'd made Julian turn him. I was too afraid to ask Isaac if Julian had told him he no longer wanted to be a vampire or ask Julian why he'd felt that way. I was afraid of never finding my sister. I was afraid of what Zora would do to us.

Most of all I was afraid of never finding the cure and letting all these people down.

36

Zora's residence was 40 minutes from the college, in the middle of a rural space of land that no one would suspect housed such a place. On first glance, we'd headed down a dirt road on a cow farm. The barbed wire fence extended on each side of the road for what seemed like eternity. Dust kicked up from under the tires as the car disappeared into a massive expanse of trees.

We'd left right at sundown after I'd spent a fitful day on the couch, trying to sleep, while the two vampires had slept in the bedrooms. Zeus had stayed with me, a decision he surely regretted amidst my tossing and turning.

When Julian had emerged from his room that night, he'd only spoken two terrible words. "It's time." Then we marched out of the house and into our possible doom.

He'd begged me to stay home but there was no way in Hell I was letting them go without me. I couldn't be saved from any repercussions for what had been my decision. And, I knew what Isaac was heading into. The idea of sending him off without being at his side was unfathomable. So, I'd held tight in the car and refused to get out until Julian had finally relented.

Now, in the back seat, I looked up at Julian and Isaac in the front seats and regretted my decision. Isaac may have only been a day old as a vampire, but he'd survived far greater torture than my vulnerable human body could. Perhaps, I should have taken Julian's urging as a sign to stay home.

As the trees gave way to an impressive home, I knew I was past the point of no return and tried to mentally prepare myself for what may happen.

"Let me do the talking," Julian said for roughly the 20th time. "Only speak if she directly speaks to you and you must answer. If you want to live, tell the truth. Jennette will know if you don't and the two of them are never apart."

"I don't know if I can do this," Isaac's voice shook.

"You have to," Julian faced him. "Please trust me as your maker. Get through this and we can figure out the rest." Isaac nodded and opened his door. Julian opened his. So, I reluctantly opened my door to join them outside. I shivered against the late December air but would be the only one cold that night.

The front door opened to reveal Byron in its empty space. It was too late to change our course. We had to enter the villains' lair to get to the other side of this current predicament. I followed behind Julian and Isaac, into the front room of the mansion to face two wolves at the end of a long hall. Their stillness initially convinced me they may be statues until Byron spoke behind me. "Those are Zora's pets and guardians. If you mean her no harm, then they are harmless to you."

The animals must have sensed we were discussing them because they stood in tandem, one on each side of a door, and slowly approached. The trembling in my muscles told everyone around me, plus the wolves themselves, that I was terrified. Freezing in place, I let the wolves reach and examine me. Their heads were at my sternum, their noses busy with smelling myself and my two companions. To my relief, they seemed appeased and returned to their posts at the door. To my dismay, the door is where Byron indicated we were to go.

Julian again took the lead with his progeny behind him. I followed with Byron uncomfortably at my rear. Being taller meant I got to see inside the room when Julian opened the door between the beasts. Zora sat at a desk that dwarfed her with its sheer size. Across from the desk, a long couch spanned the wall and was the current resting spot of Jeannette. The look in her eyes was a mix of delight and anticipation, a combination that made me nauseous with fear.

As we entered, Zora stayed seated, motioning for us to line up in front of the desk like errant school children in the principal's office.

At the end of the line of supplicants, I felt relieved to be so close to the door but also knew that, if things got bad, I would never make it out. While I stood a head above every person in the room, I felt so small. I was the only human in a space full of things at the top spot of the current food chain. They were better than me in every way. They were faster and stronger. My heart raced and my conscious threatened to leave me, but I stood in my place.

"Julian," Zora crooned at him with a fake cheer that sent my nerves into protection mode. "What have you done?" She'd adopted a little girl's voice and the impact of it was exactly what I'm sure she'd hoped for. "First you told a human about our ways, then let him move in with you." She stood, came around the desk and stopped in front of Isaac. "Now, you've brought one over without asking permission."

Isaac looked down at the master vampire and I wondered if Julian had prepared him for this intimidating vampire. I wanted to stand between them, take whatever punishment she had planned, but knew any interference would only make it worse.

"Lady Zora," Julian dropped to his knee and bowed his head. "It was an emergency. He was dying and I made the choice to save him. I brought him to you the very next day. I ask your forgiveness."

She darted a side glance at me that I didn't like, then took several steps to the side and focused her attention to Julian. "What emergency could force your hand? How was the boy dying that didn't allow you the time to follow my law?"

Isaac cleared his throat. "I tried to kill myself. They saved me."

She was in front of him faster than any eye could see, causing him to flinch. Zora's face held a giddy amusement. "You did? Why?"

"My girlfriend died."

She squealed and clapped her hands. "Really? How?"

"Car accident," he stuttered on the last one but didn't pull his gaze from hers. I admired him in that moment, the courage he showed in the face of danger. But then, he may not fully realize the coiled cobra that stood before him.

"Did she suffer?" Zora was drinking in the details like a survivor drank in cold, clean water.

He swallowed hard. "I don't think so. She died on impact or right after."

She rose up on tippy toes and brushed her lips over his cheek. "And, you just couldn't live without her?"

"Yes," he whispered.

"Then," she dropped her feet down flat, wrapped her hand around his neck and pulled his face down to hers. "Why choose to turn? When given the choice in your vision? Why come back?"

Every muscle in me vibrated with the need to push her away from him but I willed myself to stay still, look ahead and not speak.

"Because," his voice shook. "She wouldn't want me to give up."

"Boring." Her giggle was laced with disbelief and disappointment. She let him go, turned slowly towards me. She dropped her head, rolling her eyes up to mine. "He's yours?" I didn't understand the question.

"Excuse me?" I asked for clarity.

She stalked over to me, laying a hand on my chest and running it back and forth over the swells of my pecs as she spoke. "Don't play dumb, Alexander. Julian didn't care enough for this boy to turn him and risk my anger. He is important to you. Is that not correct?"

"That is correct," I admitted. Her hand running over me felt like spiders crawling across my skin. I didn't want her to touch me anymore.

"How important?" She asked. I didn't like where this was headed but knew that Jeannette would only tell her if I lied and make things much worse.

"Very," I admitted.

"Well then," she smiled, sliding her hand up to my cheek and giving it a light slap. "This might work in my favor."

She looked past my arm to Jeannette, sending her some kind of message with her eyes alone, then returned to her desk to sit. Jeannette slinked up into my periphery, coming around to stand in front of Isaac. Before I knew what they planned, the raven-haired vampire struck at Isaac's neck and drank. He called out, a sharp sound of pain, then relented to the girl. When she pulled back, his blood was a macabre lip gloss across a wicked grin.

"Jeannette will know where you are now, be able to sense you and find you. Should you leave my territory, I will know." Isaac slammed a hand over his neck. It was an instinct left behind from his humanity, as he could no longer succumb to blood loss. "I will allow you to stay in my land with my permission and protection, for now." She locked her eyes on me while she continued. "Let me rephrase that. You will stay in my territory. You will not leave. Alex will go to medical school and residency as he's explained to me over and over. Then, he will work on the cure. As long as he does that, Isaac will be safe. Do I make myself clear?"

"Yes," I barked without hiding my anger. If she heard it, she didn't care or let it go.

"Now, get out." Her hand waved us away like uninvited flies in her house.

Julian grabbed my arm as he brushed past and out of the room. We were in the car before I registered that Isaac had followed. Racing down the dirt drive and out into the highway, I allowed myself to let out a sigh of relief. None of us had bones broken and Isaac wasn't banished. All I had to do was stick to the plan and go to medical school.

We'd bought ourselves a few more years.

37

I graduated in May, walking across the stage with no one in the audience and none of my friends on the stage with me. It was a surreal moment, shaking a hand and taking my diploma. It was only one step on a very long journey and felt so small in the grand scheme of what I needed to accomplish.

Julian and Isaac had thrown a little party in the living room since they couldn't see me receive my degree under the blazing sun in a Friday afternoon. They'd made poor Zeus where a little cap and gown, which he clearly hated but put up with for the party.

As much as I appreciated the effort, I knew that graduation meant leaving them and starting fresh on a new campus. Thanks to Zora's insistence, Julian would stay with Isaac in her territory and could not join me in medical school. I would be embarking on this part alone. Once I completed residency and started to actually work on the cure, I would be able to use him and Isaac for any blood testing or information they could share. But Zora wanted them in her city as hostages and a way to ensure my obedience.

I would move out and Isaac would move in. He didn't need to keep the apartment, and it made more sense for him to be with his maker. In the previous few months, he'd already started moving his things in. He'd also gained one of his powers – melody. He could use his voice to make people feel emotions, sway them to his will or send them into sleep. Given his love of music, I'd found it interesting that he'd develop such a power and asked Julian if it was possible that the vampire blood just brought out the natural talents they'd had as humans. He admitted he didn't know but that it was an interesting thing to pay attention to in the future.

I'd packed up my few belongings and spent most of my nights on the couch while Isaac had started his move into my bedroom. He and Julian would stay up all night, talking in Julian's room or going for walks.

To say I didn't feel lonely in that time would be a lie. Julian and Isaac had a bond that couldn't be replicated. Julian had to teach the new vampire so much. They needed to figure out how the next chapter would go for them. And, I was just the human who was about to leave.

The night before I boarded a bus to my new campus was a somber one. We all sat quietly, me with spaghetti and they with glasses of blood. Zeus moped in the corner, like he knew I'd leave him in the morning, and he didn't understand why.

Isaac was the first to break the silence. He stood abruptly and startled us all. "I can't say good bye, man. I can't. I'm just going to give you this," he thrust an envelope in my direction and a flash of the envelopes I'd burned came across my mind. I took it with shaking hands. "I'll see you soon. You'll find the cure and come back, and we can all be together again." He pulled me up to stand with him, squeezed me in a hug that felt like assault, then pulled back to reveal bloody tears escaping his eyes. "Don't disappear, okay?"

"Of course." I couldn't fathom the idea of never seeing them again, trying to remember that ten years to a vampire was a blink of an eye.

He picked up the cat, held him close to his chest and retreated into his room.

"He'll be okay," Julian reassured me.

I sat back down. "Will you?" This was the first time we'd been alone since Isaac's turning.

He looked surprised. "Why do you ask that?"

"Well," I cleared my throat. "You were supposed to come with me to med school. You didn't want to be a vampire anymore, didn't want to stay here. But, now, you have to." I took his hand. "You're forced to because I asked you to turn Isaac without thinking about what it would mean."

I wanted to see amusement or forgiveness in his eyes, wanted him to tell me I was being silly. But what was in that returned gaze was resignation and deep sorrow. "I don't want to be a vampire, Alex. I want to be mortal again, to be vulnerable and feel the sun and appreciate time. But," he pulled his hand away. "I now have someone to be in eternity with me, someone who needs me, who cannot survive without me. I have to put my desires aside and think of him. I can't bring him over and abandon him, can't leave him to the wolves." He stood. "Stay here, I will be right back."

When he returned, a black folder was in his grasp. He looked at it, then extended it to me. I took it and flipped it open to see its contents. A sepia photograph of a young woman slid from the ebony case. I grabbed it before it could flutter to the ground and stared at the lovely girl.

"Sit down," he instructed, and I obeyed.

"That's Annie," Julian sighed. "We were going to get married. Our families lived next door to each other," he crossed to the window and looked out into the night as he continued. "We grew up playing together in the street, learned piano from the same teacher and would take turns writing each other short stories. We were teens before we realized we loved each other and in our mid-twenties when we told our families we would be wed." He chuckled softly. "They were ecstatic. They both pooled their meager resources to put a down payment on a one room home for us as a wedding gift." He turned to look at me. "We were going to have two children, a boy and a girl. She would raise the children, and I would continue to write for the newspaper, and we would be happy." He crossed to me and took the photo from my hand. As he wandered into the living room, I followed silently, not wanting to break his reverie. "I went to a tavern outside of town with my friends. It was a bachelor's night of sorts. A last hurrah before I was a married man. This place was known to be frequented by the seedier citizens - criminals, drunks, prostitutes, gamblers. It was the kind of place I'd always wanted to see, and this was my last chance before I would be a husband."

He crouched in front of the fireplace, starting the task of lighting flames despite the warmness of the night. I knew he must have been in some different time and place in his mind. Perhaps lighting the fire would help him tell the story. "I saw her as soon as I walked in, the women in black. Her chest was ample and accentuated by the ebony corset she wore. Her skirts swirled around her as she rocked her hips when she moved around the room. My mates offered to purchase her for the night as my wedding gift and I agreed. I had no shame following that woman back into her room. I had no second thought as she ripped off my shirt or undid my trousers, not even when I was sheathed inside her." The flames roared to life, and he stood, shaking the light match out. "I didn't think about my upcoming vows or what it would do to Annie if she found out. It wasn't until the woman in black bit my neck that I regretted my choice."

I sat on the couch, mesmerized by his tale. It was like the man I'd lived with all this time had been a stranger and I was just getting to know him.

"I can't remember details. It's all so fuzzy. I remember the blood in my mouth and a man screaming 'You better hope he makes it.' I remember the vomiting and the pain. I remember what I saw in the turn and choosing to not follow my sister into the light but instead return to the world." He sat next to me on the couch but kept his eyes on the fire. "When I woke, I was in her room. I stumbled into the bar and the bartender ran up to me. 'Thank God', he screamed, then pulled me outside into the night. 'That stupid cow drank from you and almost killed you, would've ruined my business. You go home now, you hear? Stay out of the sun and come back tomorrow night. We're closed and I'll teach you the basics.' Then, he pushed me into the direction of town."

"When I got home, my mother wailed with relief. They thought I'd died or been kidnapped. My friends had told them I'd just disappeared from the bar. They left out the part about the woman, of course. The police had told them to wait a day and sure enough, I'd returned to them."

He turned to me now. "But I was so hungry, Alex. So hungry. And, no one had explained to me what I was or what they'd done. No one took me under their wing and taught me what it meant to be a vampire."

I remained as still as possible, afraid that any movement would stop him from talking. However, a part of me didn't want to hear the details I somehow knew would come.

"They went to bed, but I couldn't sleep. Everything was so loud, the sounds of the crickets, the ticking of clocks, the flicker of flames, the scurrying of mice. I thought I'd go mad from the noise. But it was nothing compared to the hunger."

A single red tear made its way down his cheek and onto his shirt. "It was the dog I drank first. My sweet family dog. And, once the blood was in my throat, I needed more. My mother and father were next. But I wanted more. I was drunk on the blood. There is nothing like human blood straight from the source, Alex, nothing." More tears joined the first, widening the blood trail on his face as they raced downward. "I snuck next door, found Annie-" he trailed off, looking ahead now instead of at me. "I think I knew what I was. I mean we'd all heard stories of vampires. And, I'd recalled enough from the turn to know what to do."

"So, I found Annie in her room, drank from her and feed her my blood." He finally wiped at the stream of blood tears and his head fell. I saw the weight on his shoulders. "When it was done, I carried her to my home. There was no one there, I'd killed my parents, so I thought we'd be safe. But no one had told me that makers couldn't be awake when their progeny turned. I passed out in the back room, with her only beginning the transition. She would have wretched and vomited and seized and cried alone. She would have seen me looking dead and wondered what was happening to her. She would have screamed out for me to wake, for me to end her pain, and I would have laid there. When I woke, she was on the ground next to me, her arm around my waist."

My own tears broke free from my eyes. I grieved for a girl I'd never known. I cried for my sister who had experienced that turn and for Isaac who'd I chosen for and watched suffer.

"She never rose, Alex. She chose to cross over. She chose to not turn. I did that to her."

I couldn't stop the shocked gasp that escaped my mouth.

He turned his gaze back to the fire. "I went to the bar, told them what I'd done. The bartender beat me for being so stupid, locked me in a backroom to withdrawal off the human blood I'd gorged myself on. He taught me only the bare minimum, then sent me out in to the world on my own. I lived in shacks in the woods, fed off animals, avoided the men that searched for whoever had killed my parents and my bride."

Julian sighed, gathered himself, then returned his eyes back to mine. "I will not abandon Isaac. He needs his maker, needs to be with his kind. He needs led and taught and fed. That is my responsibility, and I don't take it lightly. So, yes, I didn't want to be a vampire anymore. But now, I have a child of sorts to care for and will stay a vampire as long as he does."

"Thank you," I answered. I was thanking him for so many things: for turning him, for protecting him, for telling his story and for trusting me. Those two words felt so insufficient, but they were all I had in the moment.

I hugged him and promised to do everything in my power to create the cure, then bid him goodnight and goodbye for now.

As I lay in my sofa bed for the last time, my things packed and by the door, I read Isaac's letter.

Dear Alex,

I know this isn't goodbye forever. I know I'll see you again if you can help it. But I think we all know that we can't control what happens next or if the next hour will come.

You're like a brother to me.

I know you loved Hazel too and you miss her too. I know her death hit you just as hard as it hit me, but you didn't get to go through it because you had to take care of me. I'm so sorry I wasn't there for you, man. I'm so sorry I was going to leave you too.

Thank you for saving me and giving me a second chance.

If anyone can figure this all out, it's you. You're the smartest guy I've ever known. You're going to be an awesome doctor. I can't wait to hear about all the people you help.

Don't worry about me, I'm going to be fine, I promise.

Please stay in touch. I'll see you soon.

Isaac

PART THREE

Dr. Alexander Samuel Kitchner Attending Physician

I'd love to tell you that it was smooth sailing from that moment until I became Dr. Kitchner, but I think the point of these journals is to honestly get to know one another.

Medical school was the hardest thing I'd ever gone through, and then residency happened. The years of my education in med school were nothing compared to the rigors of being an intern and then those years as a resident. In medical school, it's all books and lectures and labs. You talk about disease and patients but there is no classroom that can prepare you for what it is like on those floors.

You cannot comprehend the days on end I worked in the hospital, at the bedside, with the nurses, while also preparing for rigorous exams. I slept in the resident rooms more often than I ever saw my little apartment. If I got two hours straight of rest, I'd consider myself lucky. But, more often than not, that pager would ring only 30 minutes after I'd dared to close my eyes.

I remember my first night shift as the resident with no attending in the building. I had the pager, and I was the one making the difficult choices. I, Alex Kitchner, who had faced angry vampires and abusive parents, was more terrified of that little pager alerting than anything I'd ever encountered. And, when it had, it'd been a code blue. I ran into the room and all eyes had been on me for the next steps.

And while I'd completed medical school and found myself in residency, unlike my peers, I'd had to check in with Zora once a month. When I was lucky, it'd been over the phone. But, every once in a while, she'd show up at the hospital.

I'd made it my mission to finish first in my class in medical school, so I'd have my pick of residency programs, and managed to find one 164 miles from her territory. I'd feared she wouldn't let those extra miles slide. She'd been clear that I was to stay 100 miles or closer to her. But I'd hastily explained to her the importance of finding a hospital that was known for its work with blood diseases, which this one was, and she'd relented.

Not long after medical school, I crossed paths with someone from my hometown and heard my parents had moved to Florida. I sat by the river that night and thought about what it meant. I didn't care that they'd moved or that they hadn't told me. We hadn't spoken since I left and the only thing I'd mailed them in the last four years was my graduation announcement from undergrad. What had hit me that night was that Sheena couldn't return to that home to find me, that she wouldn't know how to find me now if she wanted to. When the time came, I would have to find her.

I talked to Julian and Isaac weekly for the first year, had gone to see them at Christmas. But, as the years progressed and the workload intensified, it got harder to stay in touch. When I'd matched for my residency, I'd called them only to get the machine and leave a message. We'd played phone tag for a week before I'd caught them at 3 a.m. and been able to share the news.

Isaac sounded like he was doing well. He'd never returned to school but had turned his love of music into a band. He wrote their songs, they played at venues around the area, and they were collecting a solid fanbase. By the time I ended my intern year and began as a first-year resident, he'd told me that his band had been signed by an agent. I didn't want to ruin his good news by asking if he'd told the agent he could only do night gigs. I figured he must have already sold everyone on some kind of story since the band had been formed right after I'd left.

Julian sounded less happy. He didn't complain when we were on the phone, but he didn't have much to tell me when we spoke. He'd taken a role as a professor at my old college for the night program. He taught students who worked all day or had kids so they could only do off-hours classes. He told me he found fulfillment in the position and was happy for Isaac's full life. However, the tone of his words didn't match what he was trying to tell me. I worried that he was depressed but was too afraid to ask outright.

This will be an extremely uneventful section in my story as I, too, had a less than fulfilling life. While I was doing well in my program, impressing my attendings and passing all my exams, I had nothing outside of medicine. All of my experiences had taught me one thing: don't let anyone get close to you, you don't know who you can trust and anyone who might get close to me would definitely be in danger. So, I used the hospital and my residency as the reason I didn't make friends. It was my excuse for turning down offers to go out drinking with other residents and for saying no to any female that asked me out to dinner. Over the years, I developed a reputation. I was the "mean" resident.

When my last year of residency came to an end, it was time to specialize in hematology. The doctor I wanted most to work with was 300 miles west and I knew Zora would not approve so I went with my second choice. He was working in the field and had published many papers on rare blood disorders. I thought if I could learn from him, I could apply his process to vampirism. To me it was just another understudied blood disorder.

It was 50 miles from my current location. The call to Zora was unpleasant. To her, these years had been like weeks, but her patience was thin. Every time I spoke to her, she was becoming more and more convinced that I was playing with her and had no intention of finding a cure. She wanted me back in her territory, but I explained to her that the hospitals there were too small, too behind in the technology I needed. I begged her to please just give me time to finish and be free to do my own research. She threw out threats and insults but did agree to my request. However, she made herself very clear that she wanted some kind of progress once I was hired as a full-time doctor and no longer someone's resident.

The two years of specializing were a whirlwind of working at the bedside while trying to absorb all that I could about blood. I rarely spoke to Julian or Isaac anymore. I never went to visit them, choosing instead to study in my time off. By then I had filled countless marble notebooks with my thoughts, ideas and what others had done before me. But, until I could build my own study, in my own lab, with vampire blood, it was all theory. The one consistent thing I was seeing in my research is that figuring out a single blood disorder and how to treat it could take decades, especially one with no prior research like vampirism. Even when I started, I wouldn't have peers to brainstorm with or federal funding or hundreds of test subjects, which would limit the study.

The reality of the gigantic task before me was feeling too big. I felt like I couldn't breathe and had no one to talk to about it. The days felt both unending and too fast. My two years of specialty came to an end before I knew what to do or how to do it.

The white coat was mine. The board exams were all passed. The excuses were gone.

I was Dr. Kitchner, hematologist-oncologist, and I needed to find a cure or face the likely drawn-out, painful death that Zora would reward me for failing.

The path that had been laid out before me the moment my vampire sister had arrived at my window continued on and it was too late to get off it.

39

I was offered several attending positions at many hospitals on the east coast. To me, the most important part of the position was that I was given an office and research lab. The decision was easy since only one could promise me that. It was in Boston, a big enough city for me to be anonymous in, and I was moving closer to Zora, not further, so she was happy.

I had saved enough for a very meager apartment within walking distance from the hospital. My first day as an attending was something that I'll never forget. I woke up that morning and stared in the mirror for longer than was healthy. It showed a grown man who had worked out most of his life, a man in scrubs and a lab coat. But all I could see was a scared little boy. I questioned myself, my brain, my motives, my integrity. I questioned my purpose.

As I cared for patients that day, many of whom had a terminal diagnosis, I knew that some of my thoughts would be with my goal to save the vampires who wanted out of the darkness. Did it make me a bad person that my focus was not with curing cancer but with reversing vampirism? Did I deserve to have this coat? Be called doctor?

Before I could fall too far down that dark hole of tortured self-doubt, I grabbed my backpack and walked out the door to the hospital.

When I arrived, I was greeted by the physician director, given a tour of the facility and shown my office. To my dismay, the lab I was promised was not private and within my office space, but shared with other physicians and down the hall. The administrator apologized profusely and assured me that I could reserve time to be alone with my research, but it became evident early that the only time I would get would be in the bleak hours between two and four in the morning.

I toured the units, met the staff and was given the badge I would need to access everything. The calm routine of being toured and greeted on that first day was a vast contrast to the reality of the job itself. I was replacing the current hospital's on-staff hem-onc doctor. He retired five days after I joined so the orientation and hand off was quick. To my dismay, I was the only hem-onc on staff, so any patient needing my specialty who did not already have a preferred hem-onc, was mine to cover. The number of patients was dizzying, and the acuity of their situations cannot be adequately conveyed. Every patient seemed to be the most important to me and I found myself invigorated by helping them. I held their hands, listened to their stories, read their charts and studied their labs. I ordered tests and gave recommendations to the hospitalists.

It was not lost on me that many of the female nurses and attendings looked at me with interest and lust. I noticed their glances my way, the flipping of hair and bending over in front of me. While I had a complicated relationship with my own sexual needs and remained confused about what I wanted, they did intrigue me. More than once, I found myself being physically affected by their attempts to get my attention. Too often to note, I wanted to take one of them to bed to see if they could awaken my needs again. I wanted so badly for the bedroom experience I had heard from my classmates in school to happen to me.

But, as my resolve would start to break and I would start to think about taking someone back to my place, I'd remind myself that anyone in my life could be in danger. So, I would distance myself, keep everything professional and use self-pleasure to calm my thoughts and refocus me.

I don't know what was happening to distract her, but Zora didn't contact me for two years once I settled in Boston. There was no way I could truly forget about her, but my need to find the cure and appease her had gone into the back parts of my brain. I was so enveloped by each patient on my roster that I'd let the notebooks collect dust. I didn't stop caring, I just cared more about the people in my beds fighting cancer than I did about saving vampires.

If I'm being honest, when I saw the disease that were ravaging humans, the needs to save vampires from an eternity of immortality and magic seemed less important. Every time I'd start to feel guilty about not researching, I would be consulted to a particularly bad case and my focus would return to my human practice.

I still did not allow myself to make friends or even work acquittances. Deep down, I knew the sand in my hourglass was quickly cascading downward and eventually Zora would show up and expect some kind of update. I'd actually been so afraid to sleep, that a few months after I moved to Boston, I'd started keeping a syringe of paralytic in my nightstand in case she ever attacked me in my sleep. I didn't know if it would even work on her, but it gave me enough comfort that I'd been able to start sleeping again.

So, there was no way I'd ever let anyone get close to me again. I couldn't give her some unwitting friend to use against me. It took a year for fellow staff to stop trying to befriend me. I knew what they thought of me. I overheard it while charting in some back corner. "He's a good doctor but what an asshole." They wondered if I was gay, had a secret wife or was trying to hide from a dark past. The last one was closer than they could ever realize. It hurt, being so close to other people but so removed. However, it did get easier the longer I did it.

As 2012 slid away, I was in a comfortable routine of seeing patients, working out and walking the city when I felt restless or needed to think. I was starting to believe everything before Boston was a weird fever dream.

But, of course, it wasn't.

40

"Oh, Dr. Kitchner, I'm so happy you're here." Mrs. Rodgers had been one of the first patients I'd taken care of when I started at this hospital. Treating her cancer had taken her hair, the color out of her skin and turned the cherubic face I'd meet into something closer to a skeleton, but it hadn't taken her smile or her kindness. She was so frail and pale now that she was almost lost in the sheets.

"Ginny," I beamed. "You look more beautiful every time I see you. If only I were 50 years older."

The giggle that escaped her chapped lips sounded like it belonged to a young woman. "Goodness. You're such a liar but I do love the lies. Why are you here so late? Don't you have a girl to go home to?"

"You know I don't," I said as I lay my stethoscope against the paper skin over her protruding ribs. "And even if I did, I'd leave her to come see you." She took deep breaths without having to be asked. "How's the pain?"

"It could be worse. I hear other patients talk about how they suffer, and I count myself lucky." She lay her hand against my forearm, and it weighed nothing. "Let me introduce you to my granddaughter. She's beautiful and smart. You shouldn't be all alone." This was not the first time she'd worried over my bachelorhood but the first time she'd tried to set me up with someone.

I pulled back. "You are very sweet, but I choose to be alone. It's not fair to someone how much I'm here." Her smile was weak, and I could see it was a mix of resignation and pain. She was downplaying her discomfort. "I'm going to give you something stronger for the pain and I think we should try another round."

She took in a deep breath and let it out. "I will take the pain medication, but I'm done with the rest Dr. Kitchner. I just want to be at peace and see the people I love and not deal with all the side effects any more. I want to go out on my terms."

This was the part of medicine I didn't like, the moment I recognized that a fight was over. I had victories, there were so many good moments in my career. The losses were rough, though. They were the ones that I thought of in the darkness of my bedroom when sleep evaded me. I'd known for a while that Mrs. Rodgers would be one of my defeats, but I didn't want to face it.

Instead, she had.

"It's your choice, Ginny. If that's what you want, I support it."

"It's what I want," she laid back and sighed. "Now I'll take some of that medicine if you can ask the nurse to bring it in." I stood, knowing that her transitioning to hospice meant my time with her was done. I envied the peace I saw in her eyes. As I turned to leave the room and find a nurse, she called out my name. Turning back, I saw her extended hand and took it. "Don't waste time on fear, worry, hate or regret. If you spend your life giving into all those bad feelings or trying to prevent them, you'll miss out on all the good stuff life has to offer."

So many times, in my career, I've seen people at the end of their lives and heard these pearls of wisdom, the kind of clarity that only imminent death can bring. I've cherished every one of them and this one was no less valued but somehow hit harder than usual.

I rested my hand over hers, gave it a squeeze then left her to her rest.

After the nurse had been sent on the mission of giving Mrs. Rodgers some morphine, I made my way down to my office. I had been so busy recently that I'd gotten uncharacteristically behind on my notes. A stack of charts awaited me and would mean less sleep than I'd usually get, which was already less than I should be getting. I toyed with the idea of going into one of the resident rooms to just catch a few hours of sleep, but I ached for my own shower and my own bed. So, I forced myself to scoop up the stack of files, shove them into my backpack and start the 15-minute walk to my apartment.

The brisk night air cut through the fatigue a little and gave me a much-needed second wind. This was my favorite time of the night, between 1am and 4am when the world is still and everything held the energy of the day's activities. It was the time when my thoughts would drift back to Julian, Isaac, Hazel and those nights of playing Raven Realm. The memories were both welcomed and dreaded. I couldn't ever regret my time in undergrad; it made me who I was. But the happy memories always gave way to the heartbreaking ones. Then, inevitably, my brain would fade from the replaying of laughter to the knowledge that Zora wouldn't just forget about me. Unless she'd somehow mistakenly stumbled into the sun, I was going to have to answer to her someday. And what did I have?

Nothing.

The notebooks were gathering dust while I tried to keep up with my human patients. Trust me when I tell you that finding the cure was a weight that rested on my shoulders at all times. I just couldn't focus on it when I had humans being eaten alive by disease trusting me to help them. There weren't enough hours in the day to do it all. I'd already cut back on gym time and barely ate, let alone had hours to devote to a cure for immortality. I rarely even thought of it, to be honest, and when I did, I used the excuse that vampires had plenty of time, sick humans didn't. Not to mention, *if* I ever was able to create a feasible study to test my theories, I'd need vampire blood to test. That would mean going back into Zora's territory to gather specimens. It felt too much like poking a sleeping bear.

So, another day had gone by with me not doing the thing that was my sole focus for so long.

When I opened my apartment door, I threw my bag onto the couch to search for food. I'd eat, shower and then sit down to get as many notes completed before sleep inevitably stole me away. I was so lost in my thoughts and the comfort of routine that it wasn't until I was cutting lettuce for my sandwich that it occurred to me that I hadn't needed to unlock my front door. I always locked my door, always.

Numbness cascaded from my head, down past my racing heart and into my feet as fear enveloped me. The weight of the knife was no match for my shaking hands and clattered to the kitchen floor. I picked it back up and gripped it like the weapon I needed it to be, even though I knew the enemy was likely not susceptible to a simple stabbing.

I took a few shaking steps into the living room, searching for signs of entry or a presence. Nothing looked out of place. Sliding my gaze from living room, down the hallway, I saw the bathroom door closed but the bedroom one open. Knowing I close my doors every morning before I leave, I knew that was where I needed to go. Every cell in my body screamed to run out of the apartment. But, then what? Calling the police wouldn't help, it would just get them killed. And, I was only postponing the evitable. If Zora or one of her cronies was in the room and I ran, I'd only piss them off. The only thing worse than facing vampire punishment was facing pissed off vampire punishment. I could still vividly recall the sound of my wrist being snapped, hear it in my head, and feel Zora's vise grip around my arm.

I gingerly slid the knife into the side pocket of my scrub pants. I knew that whoever was back there would see me holding it as a threat, but I still wanted it on my person. It wouldn't kill them, but it may buy me some time to get away if I had to. For a second, I worried that it would only be giving my attacker a weapon but that thought was erased by the knowledge that a vampire didn't need weapons to kill me. They were walking, breathing, unstoppable assassins. And, the longer I made them wait, the worse the price would be.

Inhaling deeply, I gathered all the courage I could muster and approached the darkness of my bedroom. Reaching into the dark to flip on the light switch was the bravest thing I've ever done. The second bravest thing I've ever done was take the steps up to what the light revealed. My legs threatened to give way. I think it was my brain trying to protect me. It's like my body was shutting down so I would stop walking towards it.

Sitting on the end of my bed was worse than I could have conjured up in any nightmare.

It was a dirt covered ring box, and it was the last thing I saw before I passed out.

41

It was sunlight peeking through the curtains and hitting my face that brought me back. At first, I couldn't remember how I ended up on my bedroom floor. I stared at the ceiling, trying to recall the events leading up to my strange sleeping place.

And then they all came rushing back.

Sitting bolt upright, I turned and came face to face with the jewelry case. "No," I said aloud to the empty room, trying to convince myself this wasn't real. "No, no, no." I repeated but the thing just wouldn't disappear. Without thinking, I snatched it up. It had to be fake. It had to be a recreation to scare me. The black fabric was almost unrecognizable as velvet from the mud that encrusted it. Under it was a white envelope that had been lost to my sight by its similarity to my white comforter. The middle of the envelope had been stamped with a perfectly brown square from where the ring box had sat.

Snapping open the box, I let out a wail, throwing it away from me like it had burst into flames. My vision swam and my brain tried to knock me out again. I took in deep breaths to steady myself, trying to slow my galloping heart.

There was no mistaking it. That was the ring that Isaac had shown me all those years ago. It was the ring he'd thrown into the dug grave before the coffin had been lowered. It had been dug up and sat on my bed, as what? A warning? A threat? What did this mean? There was only one way to know.

The envelope felt heavier in my hands than I knew it really was. It took my shaking hands several attempts to open it and pull out the slip of paper. Once I had, it took even more attempts for my eyes to read the single word and process what it could mean.

MIDNIGHT

Midnight, what? When? Where? What was I supposed to do? I couldn't call Julian or Isaac since it was daytime and even then, what could they do?

Checking my watch, I leapt to my feet. I'd lost most of the morning to sleep or whatever state I'd been in. I needed to do something, anything. Sitting on the floor wasn't going to help.

My first step was to buy time. I called the hospital director and told them there had been a death in the family and I would need a week. They didn't ask any questions, one of the upsides to being consistent and reliable. They told me they'd have someone cover and to keep them updated.

Next, I grabbed a duffel and started to stuff some clothes and toiletries in. I had enough for a few days, even more if I wore the clothes more than once. As I zipped it up, I caught sight of the ring box, sitting in the corner like a cobra about to strike. I hesitated for a moment, then shoved it into a side pocket.

Lastly, I pulled the knife from my pant pocket, realizing how lucky I was that I didn't fall onto it when I fainted and replaced it with the paralytic from my night table. Again, I had no clue if it would work on a vampire, but its presence was like a comfort blanket.

It wasn't hard to rent a car, once Enterprise sees the Dr. on your credit card, they offer you their nicest car at their best rate. Within an hour of my decision, I was on the road and headed south. I'd be at Julian's house by late afternoon. I still had the key and could let myself in. The second he rose, I could tell him what was going on and he'd know what to do.

As the miles crept by, I waited for the adrenaline to wear off, for me to lose my nerve and turn around. But I only became more wired. I knew that I was headed into the belly of the beast, knew my time was up. Only I didn't know exactly what it meant. I tried to tell myself that there was a chance I could talk Zora down, explain to her that I needed more time. Deep down, though, I knew that her little gift to me was a clear sign that she was done with excuses.

You don't dig up a grave just to have a casual business meeting.

I worried that by involving Julian, I was bringing trouble to his doorstep. We hadn't talked in a while, but the last conversation made me think he was content with his simple life. He taught, he read, he saw Isaac's band when he could, and he talked about writing a book someday. Maybe I should just handle this myself and let him enjoy his peace.

Sadly, the truth was that I had no idea what to do with the message and needed his help. I knew he would insist on going with me, too. There was no way he would just tell me where to go and not come with me. I didn't want him to take any of my punishment. I'd already forced him to turn Isaac, took away any hope he had of becoming human again, and abandoned him to live my dream of being a doctor. Now, he was pulled into my mess again and I couldn't do anything about it.

Taking the exit sent chills down my spine but it was rolling up to the college campus that really set me on edge. Before I comprehended what I was doing, I'd parked and gotten out to walk the grounds. Summer classes were in session so there weren't many people around, making it feel eerily calm. It seemed like a thousand years had passed since I'd graduated. So much had changed within me while this place had stayed exactly the same. Lost in thoughts, replaying everything that had led to this moment, I didn't realize where I was headed.

The oak tree was bigger than I'd remembered. Laying my hand on its trunk, it felt magical. My feet stood in the same spot they had when Hazel and I had taken that picture. "Hazel," I whispered, not caring if anyone heard. "I miss you so much. I know you're here somehow. Please watch over us."

I thought about just walking to Julian's, leaving the car in the lot and using the exercise and time to think. But I didn't know where I would be going after our talk and didn't want to waste time once I knew my final destination.

Pulling into the driveway was surreal. It looked utterly the same, he was even still driving the same car. I half expected to see Zeus on the porch waiting for me. I smiled, excited to see the furball, until I did the math in my head and knew there was no way he was still alive. Walking around to the backyard, I saw what I knew I would, a small cross along the fence. Burned into it was four letters, marking the final resting place of the cat who'd laid by me while I'd cried over Norman's death and had laid by Isaac while he underwent the turning. Kneeling down, I laid my hand on the ground where he must've laid. "Oh buddy, I'm so sorry. I left you too and you didn't know why. Watch over us one more time, okay?"

I was relieved to find out that my key still worked. The house was the kind of stillness that only comes from its inhabitants being dead during the day. I was tempted to open their bedroom doors; I didn't even know if Isaac was here. He could be on tour in some hotel somewhere. But Julian would be, and it felt wrong to peek in on him while he rested. It was violating enough that I just walked in; that he would forgive when I told him about Zora's message. But, entering his room while he slept was wrong, so I chose to be patient.

I had about two hours until sundown. The kitchen was, of course, empty. No food bowls on the floor. No food in the fridge. Nothing living resided here anymore. So, I ordered a pizza and waited. I figured

I could eat and maybe even nap before he rose. I wanted to be fueled and ready for whatever was to come.

When my stomach was full, I stretched out on the couch, positioning myself to look down the hallway and at his door. I wanted to see him the second he came out; enough time had already been lost.

Would he be angry? Happy? Scared? Would Isaac be here too? How would they react when they saw me, only to find out I was bringing a shitstorm to their homes?

Thankfully, this was the moment my system became so overwhelmed, that my emotions shut off. Maybe it was the abusive childhood. Maybe it was being in a career full of death. Maybe it was the sudden realization that I was probably going to die that night. Whatever it was, I stopped feeling all the pain and regret and fear; I just felt nothing. I just didn't care anymore. Let her kill me. At least then I'd be done worrying about how I was going to find the cure. I could stop jumping at shadows and waiting for her to snap my neck.

Dying would mean I could be at peace and that's the worst that could happen tonight. Right?

42

Something was wrong. The sun had dipped behind the skyline half an hour prior and now the living room was bathed in darkness. Yet, his door remained closed. Looking out the window, I saw what I knew I would. The moon was rising. It was definitely past the time for him to wake.

It was like walking through quicksand as I made my way down the hallway. I'd traveled that path so many times when I lived with Julian but this time it was so much longer, his door so much further away. I pictured a dozen different images in my mind as I approached: him reading, him on a laptop catching up on emails or grading papers, him sleeping in. But vampires didn't sleep in, and he would've known I was in his home the moment he rose. He would have smelled me, heard my heartbeat. He would have come out immediately.

When the door swung open, there was no mistaking it. His bed was empty. Isaac's door loomed next to me. If Julian wasn't here, what were the odds that Isaac was? Were they on a trip? I mean, I hadn't talked to them in months, so it's not like they would have told me if they were travelling. But I knew that wasn't likely. Not just because

Julian was teaching classes but because I doubted Zora would let them both leave town.

The doorknob was cold in my sweaty palm when I gripped it and turned. To my relief, someone was in the bed. I let out the breath I was holding and flipped on the light, then dropped to my knees.

What was laid out on the bed was primarily skeletal with only the wisps of hair and remaining teeth to let me know it was very real. Someone had taken the time to line all the pieces up together and spread out the skirt of Hazel's burial dress. The implication was clear; there was no line too far for Zora to cross, the past couldn't stay buried and more bodies would pile up before the night was over.

I also knew what she wanted, what all these clues were telling me. I glanced at my watch. If I left that moment, I could get to the meeting place by midnight. I'd have to hurry but I could do it. I gave myself a precious minute to stare at what lay before me. It felt so wrong to just leave her there, like even in death my mistakes were hurting the people I love. Even if I had the time, what would I do with her? I couldn't put her in the trunk and bring her with me. I had to leave her; there was no other option. I made myself shut the door, leaving her where she was. I could handle this if I made it back alive.

I slammed my fists against wall. "Goddammit," I roared into silence and heard it bounce off the walls of the empty house. Then, I grabbed my bag and headed out to the car.

Some greater power was on my side that night because I sped the whole way and didn't get pulled over or in some kind of wreck. I think part of me as hoping I'd just lose control of the car, fly over a cliff and death could take me away from all this mess. Instead, I made it with ten minutes to spare and time to hide my car. It took some work to find a way in. I don't know if I was lucky that I didn't break my neck climbing the high fencing, or unlucky. Either way, I heard a distant bell toll midnight as I entered the cemetery where Hazel used to be buried.

43

I saw them before I heard them and knew they'd heard me long before I'd even entered the graveyard. Zora was joined by Byron, just as I'd known she would be. And, as I knew they would be, they stood just to the left of Hazel's tombstone. Approaching them, I held my hands up in the air in the hopes they'd see I wasn't there to fight.

"You got my message?" Zora's voice seemed to dance around the air and come from multiple directions. Jeannette's hideous laugh told me that she got a real kick out of the joke. I knew then that it was her and Byron that likely did the dirty work. Zora would have given the orders but her minions who complete the actual deed.

"I did," I kept any emotion out of my voice. I wouldn't let them have the satisfaction of knowing how much they'd gotten to me.

"Oh," Jeannette squealed. "He's mad, my lady, so mad at us for our little gifts."

I was close enough now to see something I didn't like; the grave site was still wide open. A shovel stuck straight out of the dirt pile to the left of the chasm. Stopping at its edge, I didn't have to look down to know it was more than deep enough for me to be buried in and forgotten.

Dropping to a knee, I stared at the ground to the side of the gaping hole, seeing the tips of their feet. "Just tell me what I can do to make this right." I hoped that supplication would please her and I still might make it out alive. If I could assure her that I was on the edge of a breakthrough, I might live to see morning. But, with Jeannette able to hear thoughts, I had to be careful. I filled my head with music, trying to loudly conjure the Aerosmith tape that Sheena had given me. I'd heard it thousands of times by that moment and could replay it in my head word for word, note for note.

"Clever," Jeannette's feet stepped towards me and filled my vision. I knew she was looming above me but wouldn't look up. "He's covering his thoughts with sound." My scalp was suddenly on fire when she grabbed ahold of my hair and pulled me from the ground by it. She was too small to lift me completely off the ground, but I knew she could if she'd been a foot taller. I was on my feet and hunched over to try and relieve the pain in my scalp, expecting any moment for her to rip all of that hair out of my head.

"Jeannette," Zora called out and I felt the relief of release. But the second of reprieve was replaced with fear when I looked into Zora's eyes. What I saw was evil determination. She was not going to let me walk away from this encounter until she made a clear point. The question of what she wanted from me was on my lips but not quite out when she shifted her gaze to a point behind and cocked her head.

I didn't want to look but knew I had to.

Behind me was Julian and Isaac, side by side and approaching, with Byron at their backs. My friends had clearly been through their own punishments, for how long I couldn't know for sure, but I knew the time had been used to get a point across. Considering I knew how quickly vampires could heal, their wounds and bruising must have been given to them very recently. I prayed it was the only round they'd faced.

They stopped on each side of me, all three of us facing Zora as Byron came around to join his lady. When he turned, I saw the wooden stake in his hand. That's how he'd kept Julian and Isaac in check, reminding them that he could end them with one swift motion.

"Do you have the cure, Alexander?" Zora broke the silence, but her question only increased the tension in the air.

"I-" my voice shook, and I couldn't seem to get enough air to speak. "I need-"

"Do not say more time, Alexander." She screamed into the night and the power in her voice sent pain through my ear drums. "I have given you more time and space than I have ever given anyone. But you have brought me nothing. I don't think you're motivated enough." She turned to Byron, who faded from sight only to reappear in front of Isaac. He had my friend by the throat and in the air in less time than it takes to blink. Isaac kicked out in instinct, connecting to my stomach and throwing me onto my back on the ground. I watched helplessly as Byron turned and tossed Isaac into the hole. He faded again, reappearing on top of the dirt mound. He tossed the stake to the side and grabbed the handle of the shovel, a twisted smile growing across his face. He was thrilled by the task at hand. Jeannette cackled, Julian begged them to stop, and I scrambled to the edge of the abyss.

Ten feet below, Isaac lay in the filthy coffin that the love of his life had disintegrated in. Blood tears rolled from his wide, terror filled eyes. "Run, Alex," he mouthed to me.

I reached for him but was yanked back. Zora loomed above me, her foot pressing my back into the ground. Her weight was crushing my chest, making it hard to pull air in. "He will live, Doctor. He will exist in that box, with the weight of the dirt too heavy for him to push up. He's young so he will eventually starve to death, but it will take a long, long, long time. Before that happens, he'll go mad and try to kill himself, but he won't be able to."

"No, lady, please, take me," Julian begged behind me.

I heard the sounds of a shovel being shoved into dirt and dirt falling onto wood. I heard Isaac hyperventilating.

She looked up, I assumed at him. "No, Julian. Your punishment is knowing he's down there and feeling your progeny waste away." Sliding her eyes back to me, she smiled. "You can stop all this, doctor. The second you bring me a cure, I dig him up."

"But-"

She pressed her foot into me, and I heard a crack as one of my ribs gave way. "No more buts, human. I'm done with your games and your excuses. I want that cure. So, I can't kill you, but I can torture these two for a *very* long time until you bring me what I want."

I gasped, trying to form words. She realized I couldn't talk with her foot compressing my lungs and removed her foot to place it on the ground next to me. "I-" my chest ached, I took in a few painful deep breaths. "I've been trying to tell you, Lady Zora. I have the cure."

"What?" she screamed, lifting me to my feet. "You have it, why didn't you tell me as soon as you knew you had it?" She lifted one hand out towards Byron, telling him to pause his shovel.

"Alex," I heard Julian gasp behind me. "How?"

"I was going to call you yesterday, when I got home so no one in the hospital would hear. But I came home to your message and fainted. By the time I came to, it was day. That's why I came here." I used the time she was listening to me to conjure images in my head, I imagined working in my lab, dropping liquid into test tubes and looking into my microscope. I called on all the memories of time scribbling in my notebooks and looking through books. In my mind's eye, I scanned across vials of blood and then made up a vivid image of me celebrating after looking into a microscope.

I heard Jeannette call out "I see it in his mind, lady. He's not lying."

"Where is it?" The excitement in her voice was similar to a child in a toy shop. She danced on her feet.

"I only have one. I need the time to make more," reaching into the side pocket of my scrub pants, I pulled out the syringe, looking at it in wonder and thanking the universe that it survived the violence of the night.

Zora stared at the hypodermic in my outstretched palm. The needle I'd chose was long and thick, giving it a sort of menacing quality that made it look more impressive. "How do I know this is the cure?"

"You have to trust me," I said. "Why would I lie knowing you could snap my neck in a second?"

"I want it tested." An evil grimace spread, and she turned her glare to Jeannette. "You."

Jeannette wasn't laughing anymore. "Why me? Why not Byron?"

Zora stomped to her partner, and I saw the vampire cower. Until that moment, I wouldn't have believed Jeannette could be frightened. "Because I am your master. I made you. If the cure works, we will know we can trust him, and I can just turn you back into a vampire."

"But, lady-" her protest was cut off by a slap. The crack filled the air and send some birds flying out of trees.

"You can take the cure, or I can kill you and give Byron the chance to be my second in command."

Jeannette looked from Zora to me to the shot in my hand to Zora. Reluctantly, she approached me. Zora stood back, watching the show. I had no idea if this was going to work but I needed to do something, I was too far into this lie now and had no way out by through.

Pulling off the needle cap, I pulled up her dress sleeve and made a show of sliding the needle into her deltoid and slowly plunged half the liquid into her. When she dropped to the ground, I knew two things: the paralytic worked on vampires, and I needed to act quickly. What I didn't know was how much time we had before the meds wore off and my lie was exposed.

Zora stared at her lover on the ground, curious but not concerned.

"It will take time," I explained. "It takes hours to turn from human to vampire and the cure needs time to work backwards."

"Will she have to choose?" Zora asked, so she was buying the lie for now.

"No," I answered. "The cure makes the choice for you."

"Excellent," she whispered. I saw the possibilities swirling through her head. She probably had a list of vampires she would have used the cure on, whether they wanted it or not. Byron had come to stare at Jeannette as well. I think he was half hoping she was dead.

While their focus was on Jeannette, I started to speak to Julian in my mind. Without Jeannette to over hear my thoughts, I had a moment to explain. *It's not a cure, it's a paralytic. We don't have much time. We have to get out of here.*

Julian slowly walked to the edge of the grave, lying onto his belly to pull Isaac up and out. Isaac stared at Jeannette, and I realized he didn't know it was a lie.

Time was moving quickly, and I knew I didn't have many moves left. *I have enough for one more.* Julian looked at me, then slid his gaze to Byron. I would have given it to Zora, she scared me more. But, I had to trust him. Isaac obviously couldn't read minds because he looked between the two of us confused. I just had to hope he could improvise or get out of the way.

"When does she get a heartbeat?" Zora asked. Jeannette's fingers started to twitch and her wide eyes rolled around in her sockets. We were out of time.

"NOW," Julian screamed.

I jammed the needle into Byron's neck and pushed. Zora grabbed at my hand but was tackled by Julian and Isaac. They slammed her into the ground as she shrieked and kicked.

Byron dropped.

Julian held her right side into the ground below and Isaac pressed against her left. She bucked and screamed. "She's calling wolves," Julian cautioned.

I ran to the graveside, scrambling to find the discarded wooden stake in the dirt then ran back to the fight. They were having trouble holding her down and I didn't know if I could get a clean shot with them wrestling like that.

"Do it," Isaac screamed. "Do it."

Dropping to my knees above her head, I raised the stake into the air. She wildly tried to bite at my legs and kicked at my friends. When I drove the stake into her chest, blood shot from it in a spray. The men let go and we watched her writhe. The amount of blood that poured from her was more than any body should have been able to hold.

"It won't kill her," Julian said. "If it's pulled out, she'll come right back." He retreated to the dirt mound and returned with the shovel. "I've wanted to do this for so long." He raised it into the air and brought the edge of the shovel down onto her neck. It took several strikes, but he was able to detach her head from her body, and she finally stopped squirming.

Julian went to work on Byron, decapitating him as he had his master. Jeannette moaned and flexed her muscles, trying to move. Julian raised the shovel, but Isaac grabbed his arm. "No," he snarled, looking down on the vampire at his feet. "While she was *playing* with me, she couldn't stop bragging about everything she'd done to Hazel's body. She doesn't get off that easy."

Bending down, he scooped up Jeannette, carrying her to the edge of the grave like you might carry a sleeping child to bed. "I want you to think of her and everything you've done." Then he let her roll from his arms and into the casket below. I heard her in the ground, shrieking without being able to open her mouth.

Julian tossed the shovel to Isaac who took great delight in dropping soil onto his torturer below. Julian and I helped by pushing piles into the hole. An hour later, we couldn't hear her scream, and the site looked like any other fresh grave. Only the three of us would know that the name on the tombstone did not match the inhabitant below.

"What about them?" I asked, gesturing to the headless corpses.

Julian picked up Zora's head. "I need this," he said. "The rest can burn up in the sun. By the time humans come around, only ash will remain."

When we reached my car, he dropped the head into the trunk, and we drove wordlessly back to his house. It wasn't until we were opening the front door that I told Isaac what lay in his bed. He only nodded.

It was almost dawn when we were done burying Hazel next to Zeus. There was something so wonderful about the two of them being side by side. I still imagine her and that cat keeping each other company for eternity in some other magical space, where the best souls get to go after they die.

We had only minutes to talk before they would have to go rest for the day. I stood in the living room, staring at them like I'd only just now seen them. Years had gone by and neither had aged a day. With Julian it wasn't too shocking, but looking at Isaac and seeing a college senior when I was well into my 30s was a hard pill to swallow. Even though I'd read everything I could get my hands on about vampires over the years, it was different to see it with your own eyes.

"Yes," Julian said without me having to ask. "When you find your sister, she will still look 17."

"And, the whole stake to the heart thing?" I asked, already knowing the answer.

"Like I said, it'll stop us but not kill us. That was passed around by vampires so that hunters would stake and walk away. Then one of us could just pull it out and we'd move on."

"Speaking of moving on," I said.

Isaac laid his hand on my shoulder. "You helped kill vampires. It's one thing for one of us to do it but a human."

Julian took over. "The others will not let you live. You need to leave and never look back. Don't even think about it, you never know when a vampire like me is nearby and can hear your thoughts or read your memories. I will send you a letter soon with instructions of what you are to do next. You will read it, burn it and follow it completely. Then we will never speak again. Do you understand?"

Isaac squeezed my shoulder and let his hand fall away. "It's too much, man, but he's right." He dropped his head. "I love you, Alex. But you need to forget us." He turned, retreated into his room and shut the door. No goodbye... nothing.

Julian took my arm and lead me out the door, to my car. He gestured for me to wait, then retrieved a duffel from his car, the head from my trunk and deposited it into the gym bag. As he zipped it up, I wanted to ask him what he'd do with the head but was afraid to know. Instead, I asked what I wanted to know.

"Julian. The cure? I'll need to contact you when I have the cure."

He raised his hand to stop me. "I don't need it, Alex. I'm happy with my existence. Isaac is too. If you continue your work, do it for Sheena but not for us. That weight is no longer yours to bear. Your life is too short to waste." He grabbed my chin and made me look at him. "Help heal the sick. Find your path. Find love. Find something or someone that sets your soul on fire."

"I-"

"Quiet," he cut me off. "Listen to your elders for once in your life. Don't close yourself off to everyone. You have to take some risks, Alex, or you're going to miss the whole point of living. I knew when I met you that you were meant for great things. But you've spent so much of your time focusing on what others needed that you missed discovering what your destiny is."

He released my face and pulled me into an embrace. The tears I'd been holding back came flooding out. He pulled back. "Don't let all of this be for nothing."

With those final words, he opened my car door, and I obeyed. When he slammed it, I started the engine, and he backed up to watch me pull out.

The last time I saw Julian, he was disappearing into his home with a head in a gym bag and a heaviness in his step.

44

The letter arrived one week later via registered mail, so I had to sign for it. I stared at it for an hour before I found the courage to read it. I knew once I did, I'd have no more new words to ever read or hear from Julian and Isaac.

I also knew that reading the letter would remind me that everything I'd experienced had really happened and wasn't a hallucination.

Alex,

A sitting lord or lady can only be replaced through a fight to the death. The trophy I kept from our night was the proof needed to take over rule of the city. I am now Lord, with Isaac as my right hand. No one but us knows of your involvement.

We will use our authority to make changes for the good. She left a lot of broken people in our territory and Isaac is helping them overcome their traumas. He has quite the heart for therapy, and I'm told it was he and Hazel's dream to provide counseling to those in need. This may not be what they envisioned but he is carrying on her legacy every time he helps one of our own find their joy again. Our people especially love his karaoke nights.

You will need to leave Boston. I have read through her old files and know she had spies there to watch you. It will not be long before they discover she is no more and links you to that.

I know someone who leads another city that is far enough from us to be safe. You can start a new chapter and leave all this behind you. I've spoken to him. He has convinced the hospital that you are the man to replace a doctor soon to retire, a Dr. Boone. Boone doesn't know about vampires and merely thinks you're a highly skilled physician, which you are. You don't need to present to the Lord of the City. He knows of you and has allowed you into his territory. I've assured him you are a good man, and he knows well the need to leave a past behind and begin fresh with a clean slate. He will leave you be as long as you don't bring trouble to his city, which I know you won't. He knows about your work and is supportive. He knows it may never happen but if it does, he would use it for good, like you and I. We have the same way of leading and want only for our people to be safe. If you decide to continue your work, you will have support in his city. He is a good man who has been through more than any of us.

Remember what I told you. You are meant for something great, some amazing destiny.

Go find it in......

PART FOUR
PITTSBURGH

45

The Pittsburgh Medical Center was the smallest hospital I'd ever seen but it was perfect for hiding out. I trained with Dr. Boone for roughly a month before he let me take over night rotations. He was a character and liked things a certain way. When I say certain way, I mean the old way. His ordering was antiquated, his terminology was from the 50s and he still thought diseases in women were caused by the womb. But once I was covering anything from 7p to 7a, I was able to do it my way, and he was never the wiser. Because the hospital was small, we were consulted to any hematological and oncological patients and didn't need to answer to anyone else. And I liked it that way.

Because the cost of living was better in Pittsburgh than Boston, I was able to get a bigger place which meant a second room I could turn into a home gym. That meant less interacting with other people, which was perfect for me. But it wasn't walkable from the hospital like in Boston, so I did need to buy a car. There was no way I was going to use public transportation.

I'd moved to Pittsburgh a few months before I started my position, using that time to restart my research in earnest. With the internet, I could get so much more done. By the time I walked into my new hospital and saw my office, complete with private lab, I was ready to design an actual study.

Working nights meant a lot more free time and I didn't have to teach any of the residents; Dr. Boone thought he had a few more years in him and I was happy to let him continue. I was busy enough without adding teaching interns to my list. Plus, most of the patients wanted to sleep and I was only needed for emergencies. Most nights, I'd get 11p to 4am to myself to work on the cure.

I just needed blood, but it wasn't like I could just go ask for it. I needed to know how the blood distribution worked in this hospital to know how to obtain a few spare bags. The first night I was alone, my priority was to get to the blood bank to see how they ran things.

I walked each medical unit, checking on the patients Dr. Boone had asked me to, and introducing myself to the staff. I'd decided that the way I handled the hospital workers in Boston had worked well for me, so I'd keep it going. Being an asshole was better than letting someone get too close. I know Julian had told me to find love, but I was certain that ship had sailed long ago for me. I'd learned from Julian, Isaac and my parents that love ended two ways: the agony of being stuck with someone you don't love anymore or the heartbreak of losing someone you do.

No, thank you.

So, on each floor, I introduced myself, told the staff what my pager was and to only page in emergencies. Then I left, feeling their stares at my back. It went smoothly until the fifth floor.

First, was a bubbly blonde who literally lost her train of thought when she turned and saw me. She was stumbling over her words, trying to remember her name when a voice to my right said dryly, "She's Monica and I promise she's a good nurse even if she can't speak."

I followed the voice to find its owner behind the nurses' station. Her black hair was piled atop her head with a pencil possibly holding it together or just placed there for quick access. She looked either annoyed or just very focused on her charting. "And you are?" I asked.

She sighed. "Kate." She ran her gaze over the embroidery on my jacket. "Dr. Kitchner. I heard someone had joined Dr. Boone. Will you take over?"

"Someday," I answered, not sure if that was really true or not.

She extended her hand, I grabbed it and was surprised by her grasp. She pumped it up and down, then pulled away. "Well, I hope you're better than him. Let me know if you need anything." Then she was gone into a room.

Monica continued to stare at me, but now she'd stuck out her chest and fluffed her hair. I gave her a nod and walked away. The hair fluffing and peacocking I was used to, but Kate's reaction was new. I didn't expect every female to try and get my attention, but Kate's sheer lack of interest was… well.. interesting. I think I breathed a sigh of relief that there was one nurse I could be strictly professional with without having to try so hard.

When I reached the blood bank, it was late in the night. If I was lucky, the night employee would be inept, making it easy to get a bag when I needed something to test. I wasn't really sure what to expect when I walked in.

The first thing I noticed was the music. Being alone often, and working nights, I was used to silence so it was nice to hear some of the classic rock I'd grown up loving. The second thing I registered was the man at the computer. He was one of those guys you could pass on the street and not even notice. Unruly hair was grown a little long over the ears and his eyes were the color of river water. He was young, which made it even cooler that he loved the music from my middle school years.

I approached the desk, and he looked up. "Can I help you?" He raced his keys over the keyboard. "I don't have an order if you need blood."

"No," I shook my head. "I'm just here to introduce myself and get the lay of the land." I extended my hand to this kid, wondering if he was even old enough to have graduated college.

He grabbed it, pumped it and then I knew.

His skin showed sun damage, but it was in this perfect pattern, like someone had drawn it. His eyes, his hair… it was so ordinary, too ordinary. He was cold to the touch and so much stronger than he should have been.

Vampire.

He stared at me. Could he read minds? If he could, I was already in trouble. His eyes grew a little, his pupils shrunk. I needed to change the subject fast. "Dr. Alex Kitchner," I said, plastering a smile over my face. "New hematologist on nights."

"Rhys, blood bank guy, also nights."

"So," I asked, breaking contact and looking around. "What's the process here? When a blood order is put in, what happens next?"

"Oh," he said, and his suspicion dropped from his gaze. He explained what he did once the order hit his screen: thawing, recording and send it up or the nurses came down to sign for it. When the deliveries came, those were registered too. It was going to be hard to get ahold of one. I thought maybe the ER was my best bet, since it's more chaotic and less likely that all the bags are being tracked. By the time I left, I was pretty sure he couldn't read minds. If he could, he'd know that I knew.

I walked to the stairwell to think about what to do next. I paced the same flight of stairs while thoughts raced through my head.

A vampire worked the blood bank; it was too ironic. And what were the odds of me working at a hospital that had a vampire in it? I hadn't seen a single vampire in any of the hospitals I'd been in. But, I thought, maybe they were there, and they were better at hiding. Although, I thought back to the night I'd first spoken to Julian. He'd been shocked I could recognize him. So, maybe he was right, and I had some kind of special ability to see vampires that no other human did.

But, what did that mean?

I wanted to go talk to Rhys again, tell him I knew. I mean, Julian had told me that the master of this city knew about me and my work and would support me. He knew I was in this hospital and I'm sure he knew that a vampire was in the blood bank, so he had to know that we'd meet. Being able to test vampire blood would be the only way I'd actually discover a cure. But, if I blew it and was kicked out of this city, what would that mean?

I had made the choice to go in and talk to Rhys when I heard a stairwell door open and slam shut. Footsteps got closer to me, and I panicked. Pulling out my phone, I looked intensely at the screen, pretending to read an important email. "Doctor," I heard as the mingled smell of coffee and coconut shampoo wafted past me. I said nothing, only looking up when she was on the bottom step and turning down the hallway. From the midnight hair and the pencil, I knew it was Nurse Kate.

I heard her enter Rhys' office and their chatter. Did she know he was a vampire? I was pretty certain she wasn't.

I'm embarrassed to say I inched closer to be able to overhear their conversation. She asked if he'd met me which he admitted he had. She didn't think much of me and then gossiped about Monica's previous failed relationship, admitting what I already knew, that the blonde nurse had set her sights on me. That was the deciding factor; I'd decided what I needed to do. The quicker I found the cure, the quicker I could find my sister and get out of this hospital. I entered the room as Kate was calling me "Dr. Hot Stuff."

"Do I know Dr. Hot Stuff?" I asked. It had the desired effect. She mumbled something and retreated from the room, leaving me to take a very big chance on the man in front of me.

"Forgive how blunt I'm about to be but," I took in a deep breath. *I hope this isn't a huge mistake.* "Does the hospital know a vampire works in their blood bank?"

I got the effect I hoped for which was shock and denial not a brutal attack or the immediate attempt to mind control me. I held up my hand. "I don't know if you have mind control but please don't use it on me. I promise I'm not going to tell anyone. I'll keep your secret if you keep mine."

"Vampires aren't real," he argued, standing and turning from me. I knew what I knew and any human wouldn't have laughed in my face.

"Listen," I sat. "Hear me out. I've been studying vampires since high school. They've been my life's work, I guess. It's the whole reason I went into hematology." He turned to face me, but I could see he still didn't trust me, time to leap. "You see, I'm trying to find the cure."

"To what?" He asked.

"Vampirism." And that's the moment I knew he'd bought in.

"That's impossible," Rhys insisted.

"Is it?" I asked. I tried to convince him I was sincere, that I was on his side. He left to talk to someone; I assumed the Lord of the city. He clearly got permission because he returned and opened up. So, did I.

An alliance was born, which slowly turned to genuine friendship.

It wasn't long after I met him that I started to overhear staff talking about the fact that he didn't age. I helped him slowly mind control (now knowing it's called glamouring) the entire hospital. To me it was like the night I watched the turn, both horrifying and intriguing. But, to him, it was torture. He hated using his powers on unknowing humans. He especially dreaded using it on Nurse Kate. He saved her for last and cried after I introduced them for the "first time."

He had a special bond with her, one I didn't fully understand at the time. He talked about her like she was his oldest friend, but I knew she was just a human coworker.

At the same time, I felt a kind of bond with him. When he was turned, he hadn't been much older than Isaac. They both loved music and were truly kind at their cores. And, just like Isaac, Rhys' eyes held the pain that only lost love can bring. Having Rhys in my life was almost like having Isaac back.

When my research was ready to test actual vampire blood, Rhys became my guinea pig. He never complained when I asked for more.

When new management took over the hospital and started to ask questions about his "night only" schedule, I was more than happy to create the diagnosis that kept him on the schedule he needed.

It was all so smooth, that it felt like nothing could go wrong.

I don't know why, with my history, I ever thought it would last forever.

46

I was in my office after a particularly rotten shift. I'd hit another wall with my research and knew I was out of ideas. Looking at the table of books, notebooks, vials and tubes I saw only failure. I swept it all off the table and let it crash to the ground.

I couldn't keep this up. I was sick of listening to Boone's ramblings, sick of waiting for him to retire. I was tired of acting like an asshole and having the staff hate me. I wanted to quit looking for something that I may never find. Something new would have to happen or I was going to need to accept failure.

"Dammit," I screamed.

My ringing phone broke through my pity party. Looking at my watch, I knew it had to be an emergency; no one would call this late if it wasn't.

"Hello," I answered.

"Alex," it was Rhys and something was very wrong.

"Rhys? What is it?"

"It's Kate," he was rushing and trying to be quiet. "She was attacked outside the hospital tonight."

"What?" I asked, hoping I didn't hear it correctly. "Is she in the ER? What bay?"

"No," he said. "She's with me." He paused, taking in a deep breath. "I turned her, Alex. I mean, she's not through it yet. But it's going to happen at dawn. How am I going to tell her?"

"What do you mean? She doesn't know? What happened?"

"Something attacked her; I couldn't see it. All I knew is that she was dying. There was so much blood, her heart was giving up, I didn't know what else to do, Alex. But, now she's at my house, in the shower. How am I going to tell her?"

"Rhys," I paced my office. "You did a wonderful thing for her tonight, a brave thing. You have to tell her. She has to know so she knows what to choose."

"Do you think you'll have a cure for her soon? Maybe she doesn't have to stay like this, we can buy some time and then change her back."

"Nothing is promised, Rhys. You know that." I looked at the supplies on the ground, all the years of defeat and failure. "But I promise you, I'll work harder than ever so that she has the choice, if she survives."

"She'll choose to live, I know it." He was so sure.

But I remembered Julian's story about his fiancée and knew that sometimes, people chose to move on and didn't come back. Did Rhys know that? Should I tell him? "I hope you're right, Rhys. Do you want me to do the same thing for her that I do for you?"

"Please, Alex," he asked. "She's going to have it so hard. She's got kids."

I sunk to the ground. "I didn't know." I replayed the night in my head, remembered taking all of my anger out on her. "I was so shitty to her tonight. I didn't know."

"How could you?" He assured me then hung up to tell a nurse and mother that she was now the undead, that her next sunrise will be her last.

The next night, I sat at my favorite table in the back of a dark bar and waited for them to arrive. I wondered what she'd seen during her turn, what she'd thought when Rhys had told her the truth and what she'd think when she found out that the doctor she hated was now her comrade. Would she trust me or spit in my face?

I would have put money on the latter and I wouldn't have blamed her if she did.

I cracked open my journal and started to write about everything I knew about Kate. We'd worked together for five years or so, yet I knew very little about her. I guessed she was about my age and judging from the banner in the breakroom last year, we were born in the same month, if not the exact same year. I knew her hair was dark but couldn't really remember much else about her. If you'd offered me a year's salary to tell you her height, I'd be out a year's salary. As I pondered my utter lack of connection, my journaling became less about Kate and more about why I continued to push people away.

I could still feel Julian's grip on my chin the last time I saw him, still hear his words. He'd told me to stop cutting people off, to discover something that set my soul on fire and find love. Yet, almost six years had gone by without me doing any of that. I still wouldn't allow anyone in, still went through the motions of life without ever living it and felt a coldness inside me that was the exact opposite of a fire.

I scoffed at the memory of his lecture. What was I really going to do? Was I going to date nurses and start going to raves? No. So why was I beating myself up for not remembering a coworker's eye color. Sensing a presence, I glanced up to tell the waitress that I didn't need anything, only to see two things: Kate's eyes were blue, and she was stunning.

My world shifted slightly in that moment; it was like I was seeing her for the first time. I ran my gaze up, down and across her. There was no way that she'd always looked like that, and I'd never noticed. It had to be the turning, right? Even then, I knew it was something else. I'd known people before and after turning and it didn't change them this much. Yet, there she was, sliding into the booth across from me and I couldn't take my eyes off of her.

Her eyes were blue but that word didn't do them justice. Her irises would have put any gem to shame. And they were made all the more beautiful by her perfect ivory skin, which was set off by hair the color of the darkest night, with the shine of a million stars.

I tried to gather myself and did, just in time to see those wonderful eyes were full of hate and fear so I said the first thing that popped into my head. "Vampirism looks good on you, Kate."

You all have read Kate's journals and know what happened to me but let me take this opportunity to shed some light on my side of a few things.

After our first kiss in the break room, the night she returned to work, I knew something in her was tied to something in me. Sadly, my brain was still talking me out of things that my gut was trying to convince me of. Once Rhys told me that Sorin and she had shared a night, I knew to leave it alone. The last thing I needed was to piss off another master vampire.

After she healed me in the barn, I stayed by Monica's side, knowing the one thing I could offer Kate was to ensure her best friend lived; this I could do. Once Monica was stable, I felt this pull in my gut, this deep knowing that I needed to protect Kate.

I returned to the barn and destroyed anything that could connect her to the scene. When it was completed, that pull in my gut was gone. It was the first of many protection instincts I'd feel when it came to being Kate's warrior.

Again, if you've read her journals, you already know why.

The next time I saw her was that night in the hospital, in Monica's room and again in my office. I didn't understand yet what I was feeling towards her. I kept telling myself it was gratitude for her healing me.

When her and Sorin were officially together, I knew I needed to back off. I started dating Monica, which yes, I know was not fair, but I was trying to take advantage of my second chance at life. I've spent many nights wondering if I somehow set in motion the events that would lead to Monica's fate, but I know I didn't. I have forgiven myself for trying use her to drown out my feelings for Kate. Just as I've forgiven her for the way she acted after we broke up.

While I sometimes wonder where Julian and Isaac are, if they're happy, if they'd be proud of me, I know it's for the best that we don't speak. It's for the best that we leave the past buried.

I have Kate and Sorin. I have Sheena. I have Rhys and Diana.

I still think about the cure, and maybe someday I'll start to try again, but it just doesn't seem that important anymore. Sheena loves being a vampire and I don't want to waste time in a lab instead of making up for lost time with her. That is, when she's not in classes earning her administrative assistant degree or whatever she's pursuing. That girl loves being Sorin's secretary and was born to be bossy.

I have family and friends and love. My soul is on fire. I've found the passion that everyone promised was out there for me when I found the right person.

I guess my reward for finding it later in life is that I have two people that stoke those flames, not just one.

EPILOGUE

Rhys,

Thank you for being one of my dearest friends. From the beginning, you've had my back in a way that only a few before you have. I'm so sorry for everything you went through before you came to Pittsburgh. You're one of the bravest people I know.

Sorin & Kate,

I know I've revealed some things to you in this journal that may sadden you, shock you or anger you. If you have any questions, I will never hide anything from you again.

You've made me happier than I thought was possible. I sometimes feel guilty for being so happy, like I don't have any right to be so loved and to love two people so much.

I also know that I've admitted to some things that are against vampire law. I don't know how much you were told before I came here. I've changed names and locations in this story to protect them; you can change or omit whatever you want before you publish. But I know that you know exactly who I am talking about.

I will face whatever punishment you feel is appropriate. It's time I stop worrying about my past catching up to me.

You've brought me, not only love, but my sister back to me.

I only hope that reading this doesn't change the way you look at me or feel about me.

Being your lover and your warrior is the most important thing in my life. I will never take it for granted.

Yours until we all stop breathing,

Alex

The End.

A Personal Note
from Lena

When I wrote *Bite Shift,* I never thought I'd publish it. I thought some friends might read it and it would go into a drawer somewhere. Just writing it had helped me process some of my past traumas and current issues, so it seemed like it had served its purpose.

But then a friend told me I'd be stupid to not publish and I thought "Wouldn't it be cool for my kids to see a book with my name on a book shelf?"

I thought maybe five people would read it.

Publishing *Bite Shift* started a butterfly effect I never could've even imagined in my wildest fantasies. Since then, I've created the *Beautiful Dead Podcast* and YouTube channel, which I love doing. I've met the most incredible people, had the most awesome experiences and seen the coolest places. I've found New Orleans (my someday home) and the VAMPA Museum (see me there in October). I get to call some of the coolest humans in the world my friends. I get to run vampire panels at cons, which connects me to the raddest people at each event.

The last I checked, my book is in the United Kingdom, Sweden, Mexico, Canada, Germany and all over the US.

I still can't believe I'm on my fifth book and that people want me to keep writing. I feel beyond blessed by all the support. I wish I could go back and tell younger me to hold out for our 40s, because being my true self will bring me everything I could hope for.

I want to give all the gratitude and love I can to my children. They've become adults since the first book came out and I'm happy to say they're very cool, empathetic, smart and loving people. I have one in nursing school (can you believe it?) and one studying theater (can't wait to see you on a professional stage). While it was so sad to help them move out, I am so excited for the life they have ahead of them. They have supported me, and continue to support me, in this crazy vampire dream of mine. They've understood when I needed to lock in and write for days, unloaded and loaded my things for cons, told people about my work and never laughed at my visions for my future. My deepest wish for them is that they also follow their dreams and find the people that will love and support them the way they've done for me.

I still dedicate these books to my fellow healthcare workers. I may have left the hospital and stopped bedside nursing but my heart is still with all those on the floors. We went through COVID together and only we will ever know what it takes to clock in each day. I love every one of you and think of you, even if I don't know you personally.

To my readers, I want to take this time to push you into trying for your own big dreams. Don't let comfort lull you into waiting another day before you follow your heart. Don't let fear stop you from taking a big leap. It's better to try and fail, have that story to tell, then to end your days saying "What if?" I have scars from some failures and hard lessons in my past. I still hear no sometimes and it still hurts. I still have a little voice in my head saying "It won't happen for you." But I'll never stop reaching for the brightest stars or dreaming the biggest dreams.

I hope all of you do the same.

To those who are the closest to me (you know who you are), thank you for letting me be 100% my weird, witchy, crazy, imaginative, emotional self. Thank you for loving me as I am and supporting my undead hobbies. You help me heal every day and are one of the reasons I get out of bed. We will celebrate together when the screenplay sells and I'm living in NOLA…… *someday* will be here before you know it.

Wicked Hugs & Bloody Kisses,

Lena